emotional persecution

When Luck Hits You Hard

emotional persecution

When Luck Hits You Hard

VIKRANT DWIVEDI

Notion Press

Old No. 38, New No. 6

McNichols Road, Chetpet

Chennai - 600 031

First Published by Notion Press 2015

Copyright © Vikrant Dwivedi 2015

All Rights Reserved.

ISBN 978-93-5206-466-3

To keep the meaning of story intact, some words in hindi, bengali, telugu, kannada and other languages are used in the story.

Chapter 1

Current time

It was the rainy season. Water was pouring down from the skies. A young boy was running through the beautiful valleys of Himachal Pradesh. He reached the corner of a road and looked up at the skies. His clothes were shabby He had long tousled hair which covered his entire forehead. It seemed from his eyes that he had just stopped crying. He reached the corner of a mountain.

He gazed at skies with red, wet and anxious eyes.

He closed his eyes.

Around one year ago

Things in life are not easy, be they practical or emotional, and sometimes, we pay more than we earn to settle issues in life. Fate is one such thing. When it is giving, then we feel like we're on top of the world. But when it sulks, then even God can't save us because even God doesn't intervene in how our destiny plays out. Everything is pre-planned, and pre-determined.

The same transition happened with Ashu, a sweet charming boy from Delhi University. He belonged to a rich farming family from Punjab, and was the only son of his parents. So he was always treated affectionately by his family. When he joined college to do his post-graduation, he started enjoying life to the fullest as he was away from his family, and getting a big amount as pocket money. His father gifted him a car when he completed graduation.

Therefore, he was a person who never put in any effort to get things in life. And that was why he enjoyed life without too much fear of losing things. He had a frivolous nature and was rather "filmy". His easy-going nature made him famous amongst his group.

One day in the late summer, he was enjoying getting wet in a light drizzle in the college garden. That was when he saw Anshu, a very sweet and beautiful girl from West Delhi. Her looks amazed him, the first time he saw her. She was wearing pink top with black jeans. Silky strands of black hair touched her neck. He was suddenly lost in his dreamland and started thinking about her. When he came out of it, he saw her standing right in front of him.

'Hello,' Anshu said, 'could you please tell me the way to library?'

Ashu looked into her eyes for a moment and then suddenly said, 'I love you.' He put on a filmy attitude.

'Excuse me?' Anshu said, surprised. It seemed like a movie scene.

She gave him a little smile and walked away. He also threw her a lovely smile, spanked his head, and turned around – only to see her standing behind him. She was still carrying a little of her smile in her eyes.

'Good you hit your head otherwise I would've slapped you,' Anshu said. She turned to leave that place.

'Why you didn't slap me then?' Ashu asked loudly. She looked back, gave him a rather big smile, and left him standing alone. He also left then, but he didn't forget her smile and kept thinking for her entire night

Oh God, how beautiful she was. Her eyes looked like heaven when she smiled... Is it Love? ...No, Yes...No...Yes...

He imagined that moment he first saw her in the rain. It took a long time for him to fall asleep

Next morning, he woke up early. He was keen to get to college, for the first time in the last two months. Actually, he was curious to know the answer to his question, which she had not replied to the day before. He reached college at exactly 9:45 am and waited for her in front of the college gate. She reached college at around 10.15 am.

'Hello ma'am,' Ashu called to her. She turned back

'Excuse me, are you calling me?' Anshu asked.

'Yes, I am,' Ashu said. 'Just wanted to reply to the question you asked yesterday. Library is on the first floor, just opposite to the vice principal's room. I'm sorry I didn't reply to you yesterday and I also accept your apology"

'Excuse me,' Anshu said. 'Why should I apologize?' She sounded puzzled.

'Because you didn't reply to my question either, when I asked why you didn't slap my face.' He was quiet for some time and then said again; 'Now you'll apologize as you are a decent girl. So, I'm accepting your apologies in advance.'

He tried to act smart. She seemed surprised by his behavior but she laughed and said; 'Okay, so I didn't slap you because you slapped your head on your own and I'm sorry I didn't reply to you yesterday. Is it fine now?"

He placed his right hand on her left shoulder, looked into her eyes, and said; 'But your eyes were saying something else.'

'Are you a psychologist who can read feelings by looking into eyes?'

By now they were inside the college premises. She wanted to go, but he said; 'By the way, I also know the way to canteen, if you don't mind. In fact, you shouldn't mind as I'm not committing any sin.'

She looked at him again with curious eyes, but she had no other answer to his offer other than to accept his proposal for coffee. They shared lot of things with each other over coffee. They talked about their names, families and hobbies. It seemed they were compatible with each other, though everything always seems compatible when a relationship is about to begin.

As the days progressed, the two of them connected with each other through various social networking tools and started meeting with each other almost on a daily basis in the college. They shared lot of things about their personal lives. Actually, they were getting into the one and only relationship in this world that gives pain and relief together and with the same person.

While he was filmy, attractive, and a smart kind of person, she was very sweet and pampering kind of girl with lot of emotions and feelings in her heart. She was actually the kind of girl who took commitments seriously and would give her life for her partner. She was also very religious. She went to the temple, fasted regularly and remembered God on every occasion. That was her nature

She started enjoying her time with him, chatting until late in the night. They both started going almost everywhere together. Soon she introduced him, as her best friend, to her family. But her younger sister, Manya, and some of her close friends knew that he was more than a friend to her.

She always thought about these questions, about whether she was giving her trust to the right person. The way she saw it, if you trusted and respected a person it meant you loved him or her. We normally trust people at offices and colleges, people who are part of our friend circle etc. But we do not always respect them and sometimes we respect people who we do not trust.

Nevertheless, it is very difficult to find a person who we can both trust and respect since trust is something that gives us the confidence to be committed in a relation. These were Anshu's thoughts about love and relationships.

Anyway, who cares when we are in the starting phase of any relationship? We ask ourselves a lot of questions when we are not together, but when we get just one message, all thoughts and philosophies go into the gutter.

Now she had started thinking for him throughout her nights and planning for the next day. She believed that we miss only those people whom we forget. If we don't forget anyone even for a single moment, then there's no point in remembering that person. Therefore, if somebody says 'I don't remember you', it does not always mean he or she has forgotten you. There may be a possibility that he or she thinks of you all the time.

The rainy season had ended and the weather started to turn slightly chilly as October arrived. This was the month of Anshu's birth. Her birthday was on the 18th.

Obviously she was expecting him to make some special plans for the day, but he was very quiet and had not even talked to her nicely the day before her birthday. She asked him why he was so cold, but he only said; 'Nothing. I'm not well.' And he didn't even meet her on 15th, 16th or 17th of October since he was going back home, back to Punjab, for his cousin's marriage. She tried his cell many times, but he did not reply and most of the time she found that his phone was switched off. She got very angry.

She was not in a good mood and almost crying on the night of the 17th because she did not get a single message from him. He didn't even reply to her calls. She got a lot of messages at midnight from her friends and relatives but nothing came from the one person she was expecting to wish her. She felt depressed and frustrated that night but replied on all the messages she got, saying; 'Thanks for your wishes.'

She closed her eyes to sleep, with a tension in her mind and probably in her heart too.

Chapter 2

Next morning she woke up late since she had no plans of going anywhere. She was angry about the way Ashu had behaved on such an important day of her life. However, her friends kept sending her messages and asked her to come to college. She thought about it and then decided to go there in the end. But she was still feeling low. While leaving home, she prayed to God: 'Please do something that gives me pleasure and an actual smile at least today.' She folded her hands and looked up at skies with closed eyes.

In college, her friends wished her with all the regular words: 'God Bless You', 'Stay Happy' etc. She spent some enjoyable time with them. They organized a small party with snacks for her in a restaurant close to their college.

They were sitting in the restaurant, laughing, making jokes about each other. It was a nice and pampering environment, but she suddenly started feeling uncomfortable with the group she was sitting in. She was confused why it was happening with her. Everybody around was very pampering and caring. Anshu take this…Anshu take that…Looking cute today…Looking like a doll today…

She was getting all these complements from her friends. Some of her friends were even feeding her with their hands. She was smiling, but actually not happy from inside.

Suddenly she excused herself and went to the washroom. She looked at herself in the mirror, checked her cell to see whether she'd got a message from someone special then again looked in the mirror. She took a long breath and thought *why I'm not comfortable with such sweet company and such a nice party? Am I missing something?*

She looked at her face in the mirror. She observed a teardrop falling from her eye. She wiped it off and then saw one more drop coming out of her eye. She wiped it off too. But by now her eyes had started raining tears. She was not able to control the flow and started crying.

Why did you do this to me Ashu? I don't want these people in my life. I just want you to be with me. I need you today, where are you, damn it?

She was talking to herself with closed eyes, but even her closed eyes were leaking tears. She was quiet for some time. She realized that her crying was not going to change anything now. She wiped her face and came out.

But there was a surprise waiting for her when she came outside. Ashu was standing in front of her, in the restaurant. He was smiling sweetly, lips closed. She suddenly started feeling happy from inside, but then remembered his behavior over the last three or four days. She ignored him completely. She wanted to get out of restaurant. 'Where are you going?' her friends called to her, but she ignored them and came out of the restaurant.

He also came out behind her, leaving the restaurant. He called to her, but she ignored him. Now he held her hand from behind. She tried to get away from him but he did not release her. He now held both of her arms and said; 'Happy birthday.'

She did not reply and looked in a different direction. But then he said again; 'Happy birthday sweetheart.'

Now she looked at him with anger. 'Ashu, please don't do this to me. Leave me and don't call me sweetheart.' He left her but did not release her hand. She said; 'Okay, I accept your wishes, but you don't need to be happy since you are the last one to wish me.'

'No,' Ashu said. 'I'm the first one to wish you.' 'How?' she asked surprised.

'Okay, let me explain. I accept everyone wished you before me because they know today is your birthday. However, what they do not know is the time of your birth. I know it is 2:28 pm and I wished you exactly at 2:29 pm. So I'm the first person who wished you on time. Others wished you in advance.'

She was quiet for some time and then started thinking over what he said. It was a pathetic excuse he was giving her, but this rubbish, foolish and baseless excuse of his, made her smile a little. 'Ashu,' she said, 'your excuse is such a…'

She could not say anything and started thinking over what he'd told her and suddenly it seemed very logical, when she thought about it.

'Where is my birthday gift?' she asked, discourteously

'I love you,' he immediately said. 'Excuse me?'

'Not now… Please be quiet and look into my eyes.' He put his finger on her lips. 'Look, I know many girls, but I don't know what I feel for you that keep attracting my senses all the time towards you. The last four days I kept thinking about this. I don't know what this is, but if I don't meet you then I start feeling a bit of pain in my heart. The pain reduces when I weep, but after some time, when I don't feel and see you around me, then the pain starts in my heart again and this situation has been uncontrollable for me for days now.'

Anshu looked around. People were staring at them, but she ignored them. She was excited and could not believe the words he'd just said to her. They were both quiet for some time and then. Anshu said; 'I hate you.'

'I know that's because you actually love me from inside,' Ashu said. 'Look, we hate only those people whom we love because we don't expect anything from those whom we don't love and it doesn't matter to us whether they care for us or not. So I love you baby.' He started smiling.

She could not hold back her feelings and hugged him immediately without even thinking about the surroundings. They both left that place immediately with sweet feelings in their hearts.

They spent the rest of the day with all the friends who were waiting for them in the restaurant. Anshu was now actually enjoying the party. In the evening, when she got back home from the party, she thanked God as she'd got what she prayed for in the morning, real happiness. In the night, there was a party at home. She went out with family to see a movie along with cake and dinner.

She looked very happy now as she stepped into the new relationship in her life. All her pain and frustration was gone. That night, they had a long chat by exchanging messages and she told him everything that she did with her family.

The final messages they both exchanged were 'I love you.' and 'I love you too'.

Was it really the end of her pain and frustration or was it just a start of some new journey that would take her to an unexpected place?

Chapter 3

As the days went by, they got closer to each other. Now they started meeting even on weekends, going around for parties, kissing, holding each other's hand, sharing personal things etc. She started pampering and caring for him, taking care of his activities, started becoming possessive of his doings. 'Don't do this', 'Don't do that', 'Don't go there it's not safe'. Actually, they were going through a beautiful phase in their lives that was removed from all right doings and wrong doings.

On New Year's Eve, they planned to spend time together at a club where they could dance and have fun. She was very excited about the New Year party. They reached there at around 8 pm. But she saw him there, for the first time, in a very different mood and was a little surprised. She knew he drank occasionally but she had never seen him in such a passionate and frivolous mood. It was actually not the wine. One thing which he never told her was that he occasionally did drugs with his party friends and the second thing that he had never told her was that he was a party animal.

That night, she observed all his party friends and did not like any of them. They were all misbehaving with people and doing bad things that a girl at least would never like. She complained to him, but he was in a different state and so could not respond to her. She soon realized that he was also one of them. She immediately left the party without informing him

He noticed her absence after a while. He called her, but without success. He ignored everything and started enjoying the party. After the party, he sent a message to her saying 'I Love You' but did not get any reply. Next day, he tried to call her, but she was not picking up her phone. He tried her number many times, but wasn't able to reach her. Finally, he decided to go to her house.

She was more than surprised to see him there. However, she kept her cool and took him outside for a walk. He was quiet for some time then he said; 'Is somebody dead?' She did not reply, but looked at him angrily. He said; 'Okay, we need to talk.'

'About what?'

'I'm sorry for everything that happened last night.'

'That's okay,' she replied coolly.

'Oh please, I know that is not okay. Why are you okay? Slap me, abuse me, hate me, but don't be okay." He knelt and apologized holding both his ears.

'Please Ashu,' Anshu said, 'don't create scene. Be normal.' She was quiet for some time and then said; 'Okay, you did wrong and that's okay because we all make mistakes. But what bothers me is that you hid these things. Look Ashu, respect and trust are the two things that make a relationship stronger and these things can come only if we keep transparency in the relationship. Hiding things are bad and may be harmful to any relation.'

'I love you,' Ashu said. 'Give me a chance to explain myself. If it is not fine with you then leave me. But please give me chance.' She did not say yes, but she stopped walking and looked at him. It seemed she wanted to listen to him. Ashu said; 'Look, when I came to this city, I didn't have these habits. But when I met these boys, I started enjoying it all. I know this is all bad, but look at me: I am living in this state without my family and I've always felt alone. When I met with you, I thought to come out of these things, but my problem is that I can't do it now because I'm stuck with these people.'

'How?' Anshu asked curiously.

'Because I have taken lot of money from them to satisfy my needs and if I ignore them now, they won't leave me be and will blackmail me in many ways. Please trust me that after meeting with you I met with these people only two or three times. I just wanted to be with you all the time. I wanted to share these things with you, but I couldn't muster the courage to say anything because I was afraid that you would leave me. Please be with me. I cannot live without you. I will die if you leave me.'

Anshu was confused. But she was carrying lot of emotions and love for him in her heart so she could not stop her feelings for him and became calmer now. 'But these are bad things Ashu. Doing drugs and spending time with such corrupt people. It is not good and acceptable at all."

'I know baby, but I'm trying to get away from these people and things. I will do it soon, but only if you are with me. You are my strength; your love is my power. Please don't leave me.'

'How much money you need?' Anshu asked.

'Fifty thousand rupees. But I'll manage it, don't worry. You just stay with me.'

Anshu thought for a minute and then said; 'Okay, take the money from me. My family has deposited money in my account for personal use, but at this point of time, you need it more than me.'

'Please Anshu. I'm managing it with help from my friends in my hometown. I will get the money myself soon.'

'Oh shut up Ashu. It's enough now. You've already created a lot of issues in our lives and I don't want you to take money from your friends. Today you will take money from them and they will ask you to do something wrong tomorrow. So please stop this game because it will never end.'

'Please. These are my mistakes and I have to pay for them alone.'

'Ashu, now you are annoying me, I'll slap your face. These are our problems not yours and we'll solve them together. Now you won't say any more stupid words from your damn mouth.'

He could not say anything more in front of her. He held her hands and promised her that he would not repeat these mistakes in future

In spite of everything, she kept faith in what he promised her. She arranged for the funds and helped him. And after that, he kept some kind of control over his activities.

Chapter 4

Seasons were changing rapidly as their relation grew. Anshu had always liked the Mountains. And so Ashu promised her that they'd go for a trip together in late January. Finally, the day came when they were going to Shimla, a beautiful place in the valleys of the Himalayas. They planned a road trip. They were both very excited about the trip. She also lied to her parents that she was going for a college trip with friends

They set out on the journey together on Friday morning, at around 6 am. She took a deep breath as soon as their car crossed the Delhi border. Now they were enjoying each place that came their way. They stopped at almost at every place, to have tea and light snacks. They drove along, listening to their favorite songs, and singing them together. She got very sensitive during the drive, putting her head on his shoulder, holding his hands and singing songs with him. It was the best journey she'd ever made in her life. They did lot of fun and crazy things during the drive.

They reached Shimla at around 4 pm. He was tired from the driving because he had not let her drive even for a single second. They really enjoyed the journey. They went to a hotel to get a room. He asked for two rooms. She immediately stopped him and said; 'No, we'll manage with one room.'

'But baby, are you sure?' Ashu asked.

'Yes, I'm sure. I came with you here, many miles away from my family, because I trust you and I'm sure of everything.' She held his hand.

He still managed to get a single room with two separate beds so she could feel comfortable even if they were staying together, which she liked.

Anyway, no need to get into the complexities of the relationship. Better to enjoy the heat of the moment that was full of romance and love. It was winter, so the surrounding mountains were covered in snowfall. They both went into the room and relaxed for some time with coffee. He wanted to stay in the hotel, but she had some different plans in mind. She wanted to go for a walk on the roads of such a beautiful place and take in the actual beauty of snowfall. He could not deny her, he did not want to say no to his beautiful and sweet girlfriend.

They geared up for their walk on the streets of Shimla and left the hotel wearing woolen clothes to shield them from the cold. They entered the market. She did some window shopping – which was annoying for him. But who would dare to complain to a woman about her window shopping?

Anshu said; 'Hey Ashu, let's play a game. What we'll do is we'll go into each and every shop of the local market and see some of the stuff, but won't buy anything.'

Ashu said; 'What, are you crazy?'

'No I am not crazy, but I wanna be crazy. What's wrong in this? Let's include some craziness with this lovely weather.' She smiled and winked at him.

He had no option but to follow her.

So they entered each and every shop, as she'd wanted, and played a game that was irritating for him initially but one that he actually started enjoying after a while. At 10 pm, they stopped and had dinner at a local restaurant. After dinner, when they came out of the restaurant, snow had started to fall lightly and that made the surroundings that much more favorable for a romantic walk – a chance which she did not want to lose.

Ashu said; 'Let's go to the hotel. I'm feeling very tired. Need rest now.'

'No, if I were at your place then I would've insisted on a walk,' Anshu said.

'But baby it's almost midnight. We can do it tomorrow.' 'Okay, let's think of it this way: if there was no tomorrow and we had only today to feel these things, then what?' she asked him childishly. He looked at skies for some time and thought for a moment.

Ashu said; 'Well in that case I would've held your hand and stayed here with you till next morning so that we could take our last breaths together. So tell me what plans we have for this lovely night?'

'No plans. We'll just be in the moment and do only what our hearts are saying.'

They started walking together down the local streets as the snowfall started to increase.

They were hanging around places that were unknown to them but they were still doing what their hearts were actually telling them to. He took many snaps of her, standing on roadsides, sitting on benches, walking on the streets and so on. Finally, at 2 am, she took a deep breath and said; 'Now I'm done.' And then they finally reached the hotel. Since they were both very tired, they slept immediately.

Next morning, they woke up and had breakfast quickly because she wanted to go outside the hotel and walk around. She was insisting that they do everything fast. As soon as they came out of the hotel she said; 'Wow, it's amazing. It seems we are in heaven.'

There was snow falling all around and since they were up in the mountains, all the places below them looked like they'd been wrapped in a white sheet.

They started walking down the snowy road. Soon she demanded to have some soup as she was shivering in the frosty air. They went into a shop and asked for vegetable soup. One poor boy came up and started cleaning their table. She observed the boy. His clothes were shabby and torn everywhere.

She asked him with a smile; 'Why are your clothes shabby?'

'I had a fight with my friend,' the boy replied. 'He did it.'

'Then why don't you get new clothes?' she asked. 'Your clothes are ripped everywhere.'

'I can't buy new clothes this month,' the cleaning boy said. "I need money to repair my house. But I will buy something next when I have the money.'

With that, the boy left their table. Anshu then asked to leave that place and came out of the restaurant. Ashu followed her and noticed her eyes were wet. 'What happened, why you crying?' he asked.

'Did you see that boy and his condition?'

'Yes, but are you crying because of him?'

She didn't reply but looked at him with wet eyes.

Ashu said; 'Oh come on sweetheart. That is their destiny.'

'Oh really? It's their destiny is to wear shabby cloths?' Anshu asked, now angry.

'Anshu, understand baby. We can't change everything. You will find millions of people like this.'

'Exactly. You are right absolutely right. This thinking always makes us want to get away from anything we can do. "We can't change everything". Best excuse not to do whatever we can to solve things around us. We waste so much money on parties and other pleasures that hardly stay with us for a night. Some people wear torn clothes because they have no money.'

Her eyes were still wet. A few teardrops fell out of them. She wiped them off and looked down. He was getting annoyed now, but he immediately controlled his temper. 'Now, what do you want?' he asked.

'We need to help him.'

'Do you have any crazy plan?' Ashu asked her with a smile. Her eyes were still wet, but she smiled and nodded.

'What is it?' he asked.

She wiped off her eyes. 'Let's wait here for some time. I just noticed the boy left the shop. He'll surely come back.'

Soon they saw him coming back. He was singing a song. She went to him and asked about the song he was singing. He blushed and replied; 'I'm singing a regional song.'

Anshu said to him; 'Actually, we are from Delhi and we've lost the way to our hotel. Can you guide us there?'

Since she asked him very sweetly, he agreed and took them back to the hotel. On the way, she asked him many questions about his family. His mother and father worked as laborers in Shimla and he had one younger sister. His salary was only two thousand five hundred rupees a month at the shop.

As they neared the hotel, she said; 'Okay, we'll manage from here.' She kissed his head and gave him some money which he declined to take.

'Okay,' Anshu said, 'if you don't want to take the money then let me at least get you something.' She took him to the nearest shop and bought him two new sets of clothes which he took happily. He then left for his shop. She watched him go. Her eyes were wet again, but she was smiling now.

'Happy now?' Ashu asked.

'Very much,' Anshu said. 'And it gave me a good feeling. Moreover, you waste a lot of money on your bad habits. So promise me that you'll stop wasting money like that.' He caressed her cheeks and promised her he would.

They spent the rest of the day shopping, taking pictures of each other and exploring different places. They actually had no idea where they were going, where they were having lunch. They just decided to enjoy themselves. Suddenly, the weather started changing as the day drew to an end. They were standing at the edge of a cliff. This place was a little removed from the roadside. They were looking down and saw the lights of houses starting to come on as the night arrived to steal the light of the day.

It was a beautiful scene. All the lights of houses on the mountainside looked like the glittering sequins on a dress.

'What are you looking at?' Ashu asked, putting his arms around her waist.

'All the houses look like candles giving out light,' she said. 'The darkness of the night came and stole the light of day away, but great inventions have stolen the darkness of the night and given light again to all the houses. The same thing happens in life. When we are happy, some sudden negative waves come and take away all the good things we have in life and we feel sad. But then somebody comes along and brings the light back into our lives and we see our paths clearly again, feel alive again. Ashu, I don't know why, but I believe you are the positive wave that will remove all the darkness from my life. I adore you. I have started having one hundred percent faith in you.' There were tears in her eyes, but a smile on her lips.

She said; 'Please promise you will never leave and will always give me the same comfort and support that these lights are giving these houses by protecting them from the darkness of the night.'

As she was finishing the last sentence, he kissed her passionately on her lips, holding her body in his hands. She also started caressing his lips tenderly with her own sweet pink ones. It was first time that they kissed each other with such passion. They were not even bothered if anyone was looking at them, though of course the place they were standing at was secluded.

It was actually the phase in which two people love each other so much that they are actually removed from right doing and wrongdoing. In fact, when we are in love, there is no right doing and wrongdoing. Whatever we do to fulfill the needs of our relationship is right and everything else is a waste of effort. This attitude may be very good if we are on the right path, but if the person we love does not put in any effort to be a part of our life, then this attitude is very dangerous and life draining.

Anyway, Anshu and Ashu were not worrying about these logical and philosophical statements at this time, but enjoying the passion and excitement of their relationship. They were kissing each other without worrying about what was going on around them. Suddenly she took a deep breath and asked; 'Do you really love me?'

'Yes but –'

'How much?'

He looked at skies and then said; 'I don't know, but… Look, I don't know, but whenever I close my eyes, I see you in my dreams and when I open my eyes I wanna see you in front of my eyes at any cost all the time. When you are not with me, I feel you all around me and when you insist on leaving me, I feel like I'm losing something very precious, and I suddenly start crying without you. People may call it love, obsession, madness, or anything else. I do not care what people say, but for me you are everything. I cannot leave you. In fact, I don't want to leave you because you are my identity now. And one can't leave his identity. I know many people were in love before I met you and a lot of people will fall in love after I die, but nobody is as lucky as I am because they do not have an "Anshu" in their life. I promise I'll be with you till my last breath and even after that if there is any life.'

She looked into his eyes and then kissed him again. His monologue actually mesmerized her. 'Which movie are these lines from?' she asked with a romantic smile in her eyes. Their lips were still touching.

'Does it really matter?'

'This would've been more romantic if you'd said it with tears in your eyes and a smile on your lips, but I'll take it without tears too.' She put her arms around his shoulders and kissed him again.

As they were leaving, Anshu said to him; 'Ashu, this place is very dear to me and I'll never forget it.'

'Why? What's special about this place?'

'I don't know, but there are some places and points that are unforgettable and this is one of them. You will remember this too, always.'

'Okay, but why?'

'Because if by some chance we're separated in life and not able to find each other, we'll have no need to be panic. We just have to come here. I'll wait for you right here.' She pointed at the point they were standing at just a minute before and had their romantic conversation.

'That was so filmy, but I liked it.'

Anshu said; 'Sweetheart, movies aren't made by people from other planets. They are inspired by the lives of people we see around us. So we are not being filmy now, we are being romantic. But always remember what I told you about this place.'

'As you say,' Ashu laughed.

They went to the hotel then. Time had flown and it was 9 pm. They ate dinner, and sprawled on their beds. They had to leave for Delhi the next morning, but they switched on the TV and started talking to each other.

'I miss last night,' Anshu said.

'Shall we go outside again, my princess? I'm ready,' Ashu said.

'No sweetheart. I'm feeling tired now and I really need some rest.' She was quiet for some time and then asked, holding both of his hands.

'Tell me, do you really mean what you said today? I mean do you really think nobody can love me as you love me?' She was sounding very sensitive.

'Yes,' Ashu said. 'I really mean it.'

'Okay then, tell me what you can do for me,' she said.

'I don't know what I can do for you. Only time will tell. But I can't die for you because we can't do anything if we are dead. So, if we love someone, then we have to live, and live together, so that we can do things for our loved ones. So I wanna live with you, to do something for us and for our future.' He kissed her head.

'Could you promise you'll never leave me?'

'Yes. I promise.'

She put her head on his shoulder. He held her face again and wanted to kiss her, but she stopped him and asked; 'Ashu, think again because after this moment, there's no going back.'

'I don't want to go back.'

They snuggled up to each other and started kissing and caressing each other with love and passion. She felt a wave in her body as he touched her innocent virgin soul. She was getting more passionate with every touch and kiss. Soon they lost control over their minds and reached a place where they were away from all right and wrongdoing.

When they regained control of their minds, it was all over. But she had no feelings of regret about it and said; 'I love you.'

'I love you too, Sweetheart.'

Then they both fell asleep.

The next day, since they planned to leave the hotel at around 11 am, they got dressed and went for breakfast early. They did not talk about the night before and were behaving normally. But she was thinking about it. She was not feeling bad at all. And he was looking sweeter to her this morning than he ever had before.

'I'm not feeling good,' she said.

'Why Baby?' he asked.

'I don't want to go back. I just wanna be here with you.'

'But we'll be together even at home, no?'

'Yes. But here we can be together all day and all night. I can see and feel you 86400 times a day.'

'86400 times, what is this?' Ashu asked curiously.

'This is the code language we use and you should know it.'

'I have no idea about this.'

'Okay, tell me, how many hours are there in a day and how many minutes are there in an hour?'

'Twenty-four hours in a day and sixty minutes in an hour. But I still don't get it.'

'Okay then. There are twenty-four hours in a day and sixty minutes in an hour and again sixty seconds in a minute. So multiply sixty with sixty and then with twenty-four. 86400. There are 86400 seconds to a day and I'm expecting you to be in my life at least 86400 times each day. After that, it's your wish. If you wanna give me more time on a daily basis, that will be a bonus for me.'

'I don't know how to react to that,' Ashu said. 'But I'm really impressed.'

'But solve my problem. I don't want to go back.'

'Okay, let's do one thing. We'll come here again, very soon, and live together forever. But to come back we have to leave this place first.'

'Promise?'

He kissed her hand. 'Promise forever. Now, let's go home. Give me a very sweet smile now or else I won't be able to drive"

Both of them left the place with memorable feelings, especially Anshu. She started feeling very different. Now she was talking to him more possessively and he was responding to her, as he was there to fulfill all her dreams.

He started the car to leave that beautiful place. She gazed at the mountains that they were leaving behind as their car moved ahead. She was also looking at the people outside who were enjoying and going about their regular work.

The car broke down on the way. He was getting it repaired. She went to the extreme corner of the road and started looking into the deep valley.

The weather was frosty and clouds suddenly hid the Sun. She started laughing and closed her eyes to think of something romantic. She felt some drops of water on her cheeks. She opened her eyes. It was an amazing scene in front of her... Mountains... The Sun covered by orange and black clouds... The rain water...

And perfect weather brings out the poet in us all.

"Neelam Se Aasmaan Ki Dewaaron Pe

Baadlon Ki Safedi Ne Apna Rang Jo Jamaaya,

Hawaa Ke Raaston Par Tab Chalne Lagen

Pattiyan, Phool, Paani, Jhulphen Aur Humsaaya

Raaston Ki Mitti Bhi Ho Gayee Nam

Jab Suraj Ki Roshni Kuchh Ho Gayee Kam

Panchhiyon Ne Bhi Pakadha Hawaayon Ka Rukkh Kuchh Aise

Kuch Manchali Aarzooyen Dilon Mei Jaagi Ho Jaise

Kaali Ghataaon Ka Asar Kuchh Tha Iss Kadar

Bijlion Ko Saath Lekar Woh Aayen Karne Ko Dharti Ka Safar

Paani Ke Chhune Se Jo Mehka Dharti Ka Daaman

Khushbuyen Faili Waadiyon Mein Aur Kehne Laga Mara Mann

Inn Zakhmon Ko Seelay Inn Ashqon Ko Peele
Chal Aaj Inn Fizaaon Mein Hum Jee Bhar Ke Jeelen"
(When white clouds enveloped the Blue skies and
Wind started showing its magic then
Everything started floating with running wind
Leafs, flowers, water, hairs and our shadows
The soil spread everywhere got moister when
Sunshine started getting weaker
Sparrows also started flying with the flow of wind as
Some uncontrolled desires started taking birth inside heart
The black clouds came to visit earth with thunder
As the rainwater touched the earth
A heart stealing fragrance spread out in the valleys and
My heart started praying to the God
Leave everything behind that is sad and bad
And live like as you never breathed before)

Her heart was not actually in her control. The weather was wonderful, but the sad thing was they were leaving this place.

Anyway, they enjoyed their journey back to the home, again singing and listening to songs, having fun. But their enjoyment was tinged with a different feeling this time. They reached home late in the evening. He dropped her near her house.

After some time she got a message from him: 'I missed my kiss'

'Don't worry,' she replied, 'I'll keep it with me and give it to you tomorrow☺'

She fell asleep after he messaged her saying: 'Reached home and love you.'

'Love you too and missing you' she replied before closing her eyes.

That night, she dreamt of everything they did together at Shimla in the same way it happened. She saw everything; them playing together in the snow on the streets of Shimla, their passionate night at the hotel. But when she woke up in the morning, she didn't find him next to her. She was surprised and searched for him everywhere. But she couldn't find him. She started running down the road, looking for him here and there.

Then somebody behind her called to her; 'Hey Girl, the person you are looking for, doesn't exist in your life.'

She turned back and suddenly saw a bus speeding towards her. She screamed loudly and the next moment she woke up in her room.

She sighed, still shocked. She went to kitchen, drank a glass of water. She wanted to talk to him about her dream, but it was 4 am and she decided not to disturb him over something so trivial. She went to bed again.

She did not discuss the dream with him when they met again next day. And after a couple of days, things became normal.

Chapter 5

Now she also began sharing the depth of her relationship with her younger sister, Manya. In fact, sometimes he took them both out for local outings on weekends. Everything was right for the two of them. Their happiness was all beyond words. Their college exams started in the early summer, so they decided not to meet each other for a few days since that might distract them from their studies. As she was a person who was used to dealing in seconds and moments where spending time with him was concerned, it was not easy for her to live without him. She counted off the days of exams and waited for them to get over so that they could be together again. Meanwhile, they continued texting each other and talking over the phone.

She had already planned a big list of things for them to do after the exams. She called him after the exams to talk about these plans, but he was not reachable. After trying a few more times, she dropped him a message:

'Call me urgently☹.'

But she didn't get any reply. She got angry again, but then she thought about that time in October, on her birthday, when he had surprised her. She tried his number many times, but with no success. It was a bad day for her. In the evening, when Manya came back home after attending a friend's birthday party, she found her unhappy.

'What happened why you are so upset?' Manya asked.

'Nothing.'

'Did you have a fight with Ashu?'

'No, and don't talk to me about him.'

'Oh okay now I know why you're frustrated. You've had a fight with him.'

'Not really. I didn't fight with him because to fight with someone you need to be able to meet that person. If a person is invisible and not reachable, then how can you fight with him, tell me?' Anshu replied angrily.

'But how is that possible? I saw him today. He was driving with a girl. I thought, you knew.'

Anshu thought for a while. 'No, it's not possible.' she said. 'His number has been switched off since morning. You must've seen someone else.'

'But I saw him, I know it, I think he's getting bored of you now and wants to try out other options,' Manya said teasingly

'Manya, shut up. And I'll slap your face if you bullshit like this again. I'm warning you.'

'Oh okay, okay, okay. Don't get angry my lovely sister. I'm just making fun of you. I know you love him a lot.'

'Never say such a thing again,' Anshu said, pointing a finger at Manya.

She then went to her room and closed the door. She was totally upset by what Manya had just told her. Actually, she was not able to digest that he was in Delhi and spending time with some other girl. She felt angry, depressed, and disturbed. She called Manya again. 'Are you really sure you saw him today with another girl?'

'Oh my God, you're still thinking about that?'

'Answer me!' Anshu asked loudly.

'Yes I did. But does it matter? You both love each other and spend a lot of time together, you should trust him.'

'Were they sitting closer to each other?' Anshu asked suspiciously

'Oh come on now, this is limit. Please be normal and trust in him. The girl might have been his relative or a friend. Now behave normally and have some food. How will you fight with him tomorrow otherwise?'

Anshu accepted her statement with a little smile. She tried his phone again many times that night too, but in vain. She put aside her anger finally and sent a message to him: 'I love you and take care.'

Next morning, she noticed lot of messages from him saying 'Sorry', 'Forgive me for yesterday', 'Love you' etc. She felt happy when saw the messages. He called her many times to meet up, but she did not reply until the afternoon.

When she finally picked up his call, he asked; 'Where are you, baby, I'm calling you since morning?'

'I think I should be asking that.'

'Please don't do this. I'm not well.'

'No Ashu. You first tell me what happened yesterday. Where were you? And can you tell me what important work forced you to switch off your phone?'

'Meet me first and then I'll tell you. Please I beg you.'

'No, tell me first. I want you to answer my questions,' she demanded.

'Please meet me or you will see me dead.'

'Shut up, Ashu. Stop this nonsense.'

'Okay. I'll stop it, but meet me now.'

'Okay, but I'm going to punish you for what you did yesterday.'

'Anything for you my sweetheart, but meet me at 4 pm.' He sent her the location of the meeting spot.

'Okay, I'm coming.' She was feeling happy about meeting him now. She reached the place exactly at 4 pm and found him sitting there, waiting for her.

He raised his hand and gave her a smile, but she did not react.

'You are on time. That's really very bad. I was expecting you to at least give me the chance to wait for an hour.'

'Sorry, I didn't give you the chance,' she replied coolly.

'Okay, jokes apart, tell me right up what my punishment is.'

'Where were you yesterday and why was your cell switched off?' Anshu asked loudly.

'I was not in the city. Actually, I was with one of my friends. He was hurt in an accident. His situation at the hospital was critical so I switched off my mobile. That's it.'

'But…' Anshu said. She paused for a long time. She wanted to tell him about what Manya had told yesterday, but she kept quiet. She wanted to check further. 'Are you sure you were not in the city?'

'Yes. Damn sure.'

She looked at him, surprised, because she did not expect him to lie. He gave her a full account about the day before. She observed him all the while and pretended that she believed him. She pretended to have full faith in his story and spent the entire day with him.

When she reached home, she called Manya to her room. 'What happened?' Manya asked. 'Is everything fine?'

'No, it's not fine,' Anshu said. 'Are you sure you saw him yesterday?'

'I thought this matter was closed,' Manya said. 'And here it is still open.'

'I'm surprised too, but tell me; are you really sure you saw him yesterday? Because when I asked him today, he told me he was out of station yesterday.'

'What?' Manya asked loudly.

'Yes. That's what's confusing me. One of you is making a fool out of me.'

Manya thought for a while. 'This is strange. But I'm sure I saw him,' she said softly

'Look, Manya, I have decided to check what's going on around me. I do not want to keep any negative feels towards him. I love him and I trust him one hundred percent. But my experiences with him have proven that he can lie. So I want to look deeper into things now because I have decided to spend the rest if my life with him.'

'Anshu, do you believe he's not cheating on you? Because I have my doubts now,' Manya said.

'No,' Anshu said. 'He can't be. We've spent lot of time together, and we feel each other very well. I just want to check if he's left behind all his bad habits. He promised he would, but I want to make sure. There's a chance he's in some danger and he's not telling me about it. I just want to know.'

She was actually wondering if something had gone wrong, whether he'd left the bad company he'd been keeping or was still in touch with people who might harm him. But, on the other hand, Manya started thinking differently now because she knew she'd seen Ashu with another girl. But today he had lied to Anshu. So, while Anshu was wondering if something bad was happening to Ashu, Manya was wondering if something bad was happening to Anshu. Both sisters spent the whole night thinking about how to protect their loved ones.

This is something we need to think about in life. Normally, when we love someone, we hardly ever think that our partner might be mistaken. Rather, we assume that everybody in this world is hurting him or her. Anshu now believed that the whole world was behind Ashu and that Ashu was innocent, despite all his bad habits. She forgot the most basic things. We all face hard times in life, we all face a lot of trouble, but in the end the choice is always ours. We can choose the path that is easy or the path that is correct. And everyone, if he or she only wants it, can choose the correct path.

But then, at times like these, who cares about such logic? Both sisters were now thinking about how to protect their loved ones and were ignoring the fact that they might be walking down an incorrect path.

Chapter 6

Anshu woke up early the next morning, but she had no plans of going anywhere. Ashu called her, but she said; 'I'm not well. I will meet you once I get better.' All day, she kept texting him and behaved normally.

He seemed very concerned about her, kept asking about her health. Anshu wondered how to work out the issues that were bothering her. She continued to behave this way for next few days. Meanwhile, it seemed that Manya too was looking into things in a different way. Things were looking smoother and both of them behaved very normally with each other.

The next day, she got a call from an unknown number just as she was about to leave her house.

The call was from Police station. Anshu felt frightened. The police officer said he was calling from North Delhi Police station – which was where her college was. 'Could I know whose number this is?' the officer asked.

'Yes, this is Anshita Arora,' Anshu said after a long pause. 'But could you tell me where you got my number from?'

'You need to come to police station to answer some questions by 2 pm,' the officer said. 'Otherwise we'll have to come to your house. So you'd better come.' He hung up after that.

Anshu was scared out of her wits. She had never ever faced such a situation before in her life.

What to do now? She thought, felling very afraid now. *Do I inform mom and dad?* Suddenly she started crying. After finally gaining some control over her emotions, she decided to call Ashu.

But his phone was busy. She called him again two or three times, but it was still busy.

'Pick up the phone damn it!' she said loudly. After some time, he called her back.

'Ashu, where are you damn it?' she asked. 'I've been trying to call you for the last ten minutes!'

'What happened?' he snapped. 'Can't you wait if the phone is off or busy? One could be on other call!' He sounded irritated.

She was shocked. She'd never expected him to talk to her like this. 'Watch how you talk to me, damn it,' she yelled.

'Look Anshu,' he said, 'you are not well. You should rest. I'll call you later.' And with that he switched off his phone.

She tried his phone again, but with no success. She was confused. She had to reach the police station soon. But she needed Ashu badly, and he was not reachable. So she decided to find him first. She went to his house, but it was locked. She sat on the stairs, put one hand on her forehead. After thinking for a while, she decided to go to the police station alone. But she suddenly got a call from Manya

'Where are you?' Manya said. 'I need to meet you right now.'

'Manya, I will call you after sometime,' Anshu said.

'Where are you? Meet me now. It's very important!'

'Please don't disturb me, Manya. I will call you later.' She hung up and started making her way to the police station alone. When she got there, she asked what was wrong and why she had been asked to come. There was a policewoman to talk to her.

'Look,' the policewoman said, 'we have arrested some people who were involved in the dealing of drugs in Delhi NCR. We got your number from their mobile phone. We noticed that you have dialed their number many times within the last few months.'

'What?' Anshu asked, bewildered.

'Don't try to act innocent and tell me why and from when you've been involved in such things.'

Anshu could not believe her ears. 'Look, I really don't know what you are talking about. I'm innocent. Believe me, I am.'

As she was talking to the policewoman, she got a call from Ashu. She picked up the phone. 'Where are you Ashu?' she asked. 'I am in trouble. I am at the police station, and I really don't know why I am here.'

He assured her that he'd be there in fifteen minutes. 'My friend is coming here. But I'm telling you again that I don't know how you got my number in their call list.'

'See the list. Isn't it your number?' The policewoman showed Anshu the call log of one of the people whom they'd arrested.

'Yes, it's my number,' Anshu said. "But I really don't how it is there.'

'Tell me how many times you take drugs a day,' the policewoman asked.

'Excuse me, I belong to a good and cultured family!'

'Okay. You also seem to be educated. But if you are educated then, I believe you can see your number appearing in the call log of one of the persons who were arrested. And yet you are still saying you don't know how that is. Either you are insane or you have taken drugs today with breakfast – because these people deal in bloody drugs that are consumed by youngsters like you.'

Now Anshu was not able to answer properly and the fear was showing in her eyes, because the policewoman was technically not wrong. But just then Ashu reached the station, and she started weeping when she saw him. He held her in his arms and she soon started crying loudly and put her head on his chest. He consoled her and asked her to sit in a corner. She sat on a bench while he spoke with some police officers outside. She was not feeling at all comfortable, but then who could possibly feel comfortable in such circumstances?

He came to her after sometime. 'Let's go,' he said.

'What happened?' she asked him 'What's all this about?'

'Let's get out of here first, and then we'll talk.' They left that place. She wanted to get out there as soon as possible too anyway. When they got out, she took a deep, long breath, her eyes closed. 'Ashu, could you tell me what's going on?' she asked.

'Look it's all because of me. I want to say sorry for all this.'
'Because of you?'

'You don't know about this. One day, I wanted to call them because they were calling me. And since there were some issues with my mobile, I took your cell and called them.'

'What?'

'Yes. That's the truth. Can't I use your things?'

'Look Ashu, I love you and yes, you can use my things. I won't even ask why you used my mobile without telling me. The thing is, you said you called one or two times. But there were lots of calls that were dialed from my mobile to that number. On many different days. That's the issue here.'

'Yes one or two doesn't always literally mean one or two. It may be more than that.'

'Okay. Leave this. But tell me, you promised me you'll never interact with these people again. But you did. Why?"

'Oh come on, Anshu. Please don't behave like my mom. You are my girlfriend. So act like that. I'm tense as it is.'

'Okay,' she said. "I am your girlfriend and I'll act like that. So then isn't it your responsibility to look after me?'

'I said I'm sorry for all this.'

'No, it's not about saying sorry and I'm not asking why you used my mobile. I am not even angry that I had to go to the police station. Because I believe if we are going to be together, then we have to share and accept each other's negative points too. That is our responsibility. We cannot accept only the positive traits of a person and leave him because of his negative traits. If we want to enjoy the good things about someone, then we should also have courage to adjust to the negative aspects of the same person.

'Okay then,' Ashu said. "Tell me when you think we should leave someone and walk out of a relationship.'

'Only in two cases. One, in case of betrayal and, secondly, in case the other person is not committed to the relationship and shows no interest in making the relation last and wants the relation to continue only for the time being.'

'But then, miss philosopher, tell me how you'll leave a person who is betraying over you, given that he has already left you.'

'The one who betrays, the one who runs away from the commitments of a relationship, can't be forgiven by God. Sooner or later they'll realize their mistake and come back to the same person they betrayed or ran away from. If they get them again, they are lucky. But, most of the time, we don't get people a second time.'

'According to you, what's more dangerous? To betray or to run away from commitment?'

'Betrayal may be murderous, and if it is not, then it might be worse even. And running away from commitments won't cause such severe consequences. But will have to be paid for.'

He thought for a while and then he laughed. 'Please tell me where you got all this nonsense from. What books are you reading nowadays? I think you are reading too many spiritual books. Okay, leave it. I am getting very hungry now and if you do not take me for lunch, I think I'll eat you.'

'Hello, this is not nonsense, this is practicality,' Anshu said.

'Okay, but let's not think about all this now. Right now I am hungry. Please make me happy with some spicy food. Or else I will eat you, my sweet intelligent baby.'

He held her in his arms. They had a good laugh and then went to have lunch at a restaurant. Nevertheless, her question as to why he'd broken his promise by meeting those bad people remained unanswered. They went for lunch, enjoyed the food, spent some lovely time together and then he finally dropped her near her house in the evening.

Chapter 7

When she got home in the evening, Manya asked to talk to her alone, to discuss something urgent.

'Where were you all day? Don't tell me you were with Ashu.'

Anshu told her "What happened and yes, I was with him. But what's the problem?'

Manya paused and took a deep breath. 'Anshu, if I tell you to leave him, what would you say?'

'What?'

'Please answer me. If I ask you to leave him, what would you do?'

'I'll ask you why,' Anshu said after a long silence.

'Anshu,' Manya said, 'he is betraying you.'

'Manya, I'll slap you,' Anshu said angrily. 'I'm not in a position to listen to such disgusting things, so please stop this nonsense.'

'Sit down and listen to me carefully,' Manya said. 'Last week, after I saw him with another girl and he lied to you, I decided to investigate. I played a simple game. I gave his number to one of my best friends. Her name is Sakshi. She met me in the gym. I asked her to call him as a credit card company girl who sells credit cards.'

'What is this shit? Are you doubting him and following him, Manya? This is cheap and disgusting. You know I've decided to have a long term relation with him and you are doing all these things?'

'Yes I know you have decided to settle down with him and that's why I am doing these things. Now listen, Sakshi has been calling him for the last few days, and he has taken an interest in talking to her. They exchanged numbers. Believe it or not, the number he gave her is different number from what you have. He now talks to her from that number. Not only that, he had also been insisting her to meet. She has refused him for now.'

'Look I don't trust any of this,' Anshu said. 'and I don't want to listen anything bad you have to say about him.'

'Okay. Don't do anything. Just wait and see what happens. Let things go on as they are and see the result.

'What do you mean?'

'I mean let Sakshi handle this her way and see what happens. If he is sincere, then he will come clean about this, but if he is not, then....'

'Then?'

'Look Anshu, you love him. That is good. In love and relationships, having blind trust is acceptable, but closing your eyes is not. It may hurt you. In fact it will hurt you.' And with that, she left the room.

Anshu was confused by what Manya said. During dinner, she thought a lot about what Manya had told her and, after dinner, she said to Manya; 'Look, you do what you want to, but I believe he's not flirting behind my back because I feel him around me all the time. Let me know what happens when you finish all your drama.'

'Okay. Thanks for this, but please come to me in future whenever I ask you to come. I love you and that's why I'm doing all this drama.'

Anshu was not able to sleep in the night. So much had happened in her life that day. She had a full faith in Ashu. In the night, she texted him for some time and then slept.

Next day, during breakfast, she realized how yesterday, when she asked him about breaking his promise and meeting those bad boys again, he had smartly changed the subject. Her question remained unanswered. She immediately sent a message to him: 'When to meet today?'

Ashu replied: 'I am busy and will meet you in the evening at 4.'

She replied: 'Okay☺.'

They met in the evening as planned. She behaved normally during their meeting and after a while started talking about yesterday's events. 'I was thinking about yesterday and it seems to me that the whole event was very wrong.'

'I agree with you, but I thought that chapter was closed.' 'Ashu, you have a bad habit of closing things in between.' 'And you have a bad habit of taking issues too far,' he immediately countered.

'What, are you saying that I created an issue that could have been avoided?'

'I think so.'

'You are completely wrong, Ashu. Did I ask you why you used my mobile to call those bad people? I did not even think about it. My only concern was why you didn't stop meeting those bad people. You made a promise and broke it. I always say that if you promise then you must make good on it. And if you cannot make good on it, then no need to promise. Because a promise gives a hope to the recipient, and if you fail to make good on it then hope ends. And when hope ends, then life becomes hell. But you won't understand this as you don't believe in these things.'

'Look Anshu, you have to trust me.'

'I trust over you blindly, but I can't close my eyes. And tell me one more thing, why do you always run away from discussions? If we are together, then we should have a discussion about the things that are going wrong around us. And whatever happened yesterday was wrong. I am still not thinking about what went wrong with me. I am more concerned about things that may impact you.'

'Okay then please think about yourself and not about me. I'll take care of my own life.'

'No, we both have to think about each other. It's you who can think for my benefit more than anybody else, except my family. And it's me who can think for you in a similar way as we love and care for each other. However, if you don't understand this, then there is no way to have any discussion on this topic. We'll meet once you realize all your mistakes and can change your behavior. Till then, I think we should give each other some space so that you can think better.'

She said that and left. She decided now that he had to learn his lesson. His behavior was not acceptable. He was continuously displaying ignorant behavior and his approach towards life and relationships was pathetic.

She was hurt by his behavior because, in her opinion, he should have understood her. But then, again, he was completely ignorant.

Only those who have the courage to take their relationship to the next level have face-to-face discussions. People who avoid it, who do not care much for eye contact and/or move their eyes around while having serious discussion, actually have no courage to take the relationship to next level and we should leave these people immediately as they can leave us anytime, anywhere, and in any situation owing to their fake reasons, ego, self-respect, and attitude. Every person who leaves a relationship has his or her own perceptions of why he or she is doing it and thinks that his or her reasons are good, so we cannot argue.

Anyway, Anshu too was thinking in a similar way at this time and was in the process of taking a decision about her relationship. She came back home in a different mood, thinking about what had happened today. She realized that he hadn't even called out and tried to stop her.

Is he the same person with whom I spent so much time with and with whom I shared every moment and every emotion of my life?

She was feeling bad because he did not try to stop her and didn't even call her or message her even once. She thought again about what had happened and felt bad. Nevertheless, she took a decision now to not call or message him as she wanted him to be mature.

She was not breaking up with him. She just wanted to give him some space for some time to think.

This time she was firmly decided not to contact him until he realized his blunders. She did not call him, but she waited, hoping with all her heart that he would call or at least a message. She checked her mobile every minute to see if there was something there that could make her happy.

However, the irony is that we get surprises when we least expect them and don't get anything when we do in fact start expecting them.

Chapter 8

After a few days, Anshu became more miserable. She started missing Ashu badly. She tried not to think about him by doing things like listening to music, talking to her friends, watching her favorite movies, going to the temple to meditate and so on. But then, when the heart misses someone, nothing seems fun or interesting. If the person we miss is not with us, nothing can give us peace. Lot of people can tell us to go ahead in life and to keep moving. They can tell us that nothing is forever, and to believe in ourselves and to leave those who don't care for us. They can ask; 'Why waste tears for those who doesn't deserve it?' and tell us that the one who will deserve those tears will not let us cry.

The fight between heart and mind is always a complex one. Anshu started suffering from heartache. She lost her appetite. She started getting irritated with family for everything. Her rather pathetic condition was plain for everyone, connected to her, be they family or friends, to see. Her condition changed drastically in a period of only three weeks.

What's going on and what is going to happen?

This is again one of the most irritating phases of life wherein we feel isolated from everyone around us. We execrate our feelings and the person who has created such a situation for us but, in vain. It gives us relief for a moment, but the same pain, irritation, and frustration start again after some time.

One afternoon Manya sent Anshu a message saying; 'I need to discuss something urgently. It is very important.'

Anshu replied: 'What happened?'

Manya replied: 'I'll talk to you in the evening.'

In the evening, when Manya came in, Anshu asked her; 'Now tell me what you wanted to discuss.'

'Look Anshu,' Manya said, 'first of all, you have to promise me that you won't feel bad after our discussion and that you'll listen to me carefully. It is about Ashu, so I'm assuming you will behave stupidly.'

'Manya, please don't lecture me and tell me what the issue is. I'm mature enough to handle any situation.'

Manya went quiet for a moment then said; 'Anshu, leave him. He is betraying you.'

'Manya, be specific and clear. Don't say vague things.'
'Anshu, isn't this clear and specific enough for you? I'm telling you to leave him.'

'Could you please tell me what the issue is? Now you are irritating me.'

'Okay, you know my friend Sakshi right? The one whom I asked to talk to him?'

'Yes I know. What about her?'

'I've been watching you these past three weeks. You're in a situation I never expected you to get into. Not just me, everyone in the family is talking about you and your situation. Go to the washroom and look at your face and eyes in the mirror. You are looking pathetic.'

'Oh come on, Manya. Please don't tell me about how I look. Tell me what the issue is!'

'Okay, now listen… Sakshi and Ashu have been dating for the last ten days. Is this enough for you to leave him?'

Anshu just stared for a while, not fully comprehending what she's just heard..

'Hello?' Manya said. 'What happened?'

'How… How can you say that?'

'Because that's what my friend is telling me.'

'Look, Manya, I don't believe any of this. You trust your friend. And I trust my boyfriend and love. We had some fight, but that doesn't mean the trust is gone.'

'What the hell is wrong with you? You are not getting my point, Are you crazy? I don't know what to tell you. I don't know whether to cry or laugh!'

'You don't react and don't do anything. Please just leave me alone.'

'Anshu, you'd better remember this. I will not let you destroy your life yourself!'

'I am with him and that's it,' Anshu said.

'Anshu, I always supported you when you were going around with him. I liked that you were in a relationship, but now I know that this is something that will destroy your life. And I will not let that happen.'

Anshu took a deep breath. 'Manya –'

But Manya cut her off. "No, I don't want to listen to anything from you. I am telling you something, but you're not believing it. I am your damn sister and I've already told you that, in love and relationships, it is good to have blind trust, but it is not wise to close your eyes. You will fall in a deep valley and there will be no coming out of it.' She said this very angrily

'Okay,' Anshu said, 'let me call him and ask what's going on and whether whatever you are saying is true.'

'Anshu, don't be a fool. Do you really think he's going to say "Yes I am betraying you" when you ask him. He'll have another story to fool you.'

Anshu started to dial his number but Manya forcefully took her cell away. 'Anshu, okay, if you don't trust me, then don't. But let me prove it. You keep trusting him. I will prove that he is not trustworthy. But for that you will have to cooperate with me for a few days. Please, it's a request.'

Anshu thought about it for some time. 'Okay, but if you are wrong then I'll never speak to you again.'

'Okay,' Manya said. 'But until then, you must do what I tell you.'

'Okay, done,' Anshu said. And then Manya left the room.

She spent the next few days feeling very confused. After three days, Manya asked her to be at home because she had called Sakshi to come over and discuss something important. Sakshi came and Manya introduced Sakshi to her family and then to Anshu. After all the formalities, they went to the bedroom.

'Okay,' Anshu said, 'now you both tell me what's going on and, first of all, tell me why she –' she pointed at Sakshi '– is helping me. Because I've been curious from the beginning about why she's been doing all these cheap things and going around with someone else's boyfriend.'

Sakshi only smiled. 'I believe that cheap things and people should only be handled cheaply.'

She had a point because it is always difficult to understand how things should be handled. Some good people say; 'If somebody wrongs, you then pay him back for all the good things he did so that he can change his perception.' But some people say; 'If a person is bad, then he cannot change his perception by just getting good things. Rather, he or she will do even more bad things to you then.'

People change continuously and drastically in their attitudes, perceptions, and behavior for no reason. And, sometimes, we do not change no matter what happens. Therefore, human nature is unpredictable and the one who can predict the behavior of people can only be a god or an alien.

Anyway, Sakshi's worldview was simple – If somebody is doing wrong by you, then you should make them pay.

'What?' Anshu demanded. 'Who is cheap?'

'Didn't you get what I said?' Sakshi said.

'No.'

'Then I feel sorry for you. If you're not getting what I'm saying, then you are a fool. And if you *do* get what I'm saying and are just ignoring my words, then you are an even bigger fool.'

'Who the hell do you think you are to talk to me like this?' asked Anshu angrily.

Manya intervened saying; 'Okay, okay, okay. I think we should just have a straightforward discussion here. Look Anshu, Sakshi is my friend and you should behave properly with her. After all, she is helping us and nothing else. Now I think we should get to the point rather than getting into these useless fights and discussions.'

Sakshi said; 'And one more thing Anshu. Manya has discussed everything with me and I'm sorry, but I have spent a lot of time with your boyfriend these past few days. I can understand what's going on in your mind, but I would still request you to please listen to everything I'm saying very carefully because this is your life we're talking about here and nothing else.'

'Okay,' Anshu said, 'if it is a matter of my life, why do you care so much about it?'

'Because, a few months ago, I faced the same situation you are currently facing. That's why. I can understand this pain that makes it hard to even breathe. I decided then that I'm going to help people who trust and love someone and only get betrayal in return. I know that at this point of time you'll hardly believe me, but you need to have some patience.'

Anshu said to Sakshi; 'Okay, tell me what's going on.'

'Look Anshu,' Sakshi said, 'As I've already told you, cheap things have to be handled cheaply. When Manya told me about your problems, I knew at once that you would not listen to her if she asked you to leave your boyfriend. Even I think that you should not do it, because we should never give up on our relationships just because some other person suggests it. That is not fair to the relationship to which you have given everything. I see some people breaking up through messages and calls and some people who send others to break terms for them. This is really pathetic and immature behavior. When we start a relationship, we behave as if we can't live without the other person. We spend lots of days, nights, months, and seconds together and enjoy a lot of great moments – lots of kisses when we are together and, when we are not together, lots of planning about marriage and life after that through messages and chats.

'However, after a few days, it's all over for some reason. I don't understand why people get into relationships just to get a taste of them and then, when the time comes to take the relation to the next level, they suddenly need permissions from a third person. Do they ask for permission from anyone before they get into a relation or before they say 'I love you' for the first time or before their first kiss or before they plan for marriage and life after marriage? No. But to fulfill their dreams they need permission from their family, friends, and even God sometimes. If they get permission, then fine, but if they don't, then they try to find reasons to break up and start looking at the negative traits of their partners. And, since nobody is perfect, they immediately find negative points and then shift their focus to those traits only. They forget the millions of good moments they spent together. They forget that, to live together, we need only one thing and that is the *desire* to live together. Everyone has positive and negative trait. The point is what you want to focus on'

As Sakshi completed her speech, a tear dripped out of her eye.

There was a complete silence in the room. After listening to what Sakshi said, Anshu started feeling differently. She started thinking deeply about what she'd just heard. She said; 'Sakshi, I am really sorry about your relationship and… I don't know what to say…'

"Don't be,' Sakshi said, cutting Anshu off. 'Please don't apologize to anyone, because that in itself cannot give relief. Mark my words. In life, don't leave your love, and if your love betrays you, then don't leave such a betrayer. This rule applies to everyone, both boys and girls. So, in your case, I am sorry, but he is betraying you and you have to get away from him as soon as possible – but not in the way people normally do. There has to be a different way. You will do it, *we* will do it, and it will be something he will never forget. Believe me.' She said all this with passion in her eyes

'Look, as far as my things are concerned, I need to think over it,' Anshu said.

'Yes, you won't need to do anything. You will take action only once it is all proved to you. We'll do it all. We just need your cooperation.'

'Okay, fine, I'll cooperate.' Anshu smiled a little at her and then they went to eat something.

That night, she thought over what Sakshi had told her. Sakshi's words had really touched her heart. She started thinking about what had gone wrong with Sakshi's personal life and about how she had behaved with her today. She felt sorry for her and sent her a message saying; 'I'm really sorry for my behavior today. I'm actually not a bad-mannered girl, but right now things are not good in my life so I just lost patience. Sorry if I hurt you. In fact, I know I hurt you☹'

'No problem,' Sakshi replied. 'I understand the place you are in. I have gone through the same so no issues. Take care. And be happy☺'

Anshu could not sleep that night for a long time. She lay awake thinking about Sakshi and life.

Chapter 9

The next morning, when Anshu woke up, she checked her mobile to see whether anything had come from his side. It had become routine for her to check her mobile for calls or messages from him. She forgot what happened last night and started thinking about her time with him. Again she ate a little breakfast, felt isolated, desolate, wanted to get out of the house and sit at any metro station, put on her earphones and listen to sad songs or sit at any shopping mall to think over what had gone wrong and how to solve it.

Going to the places she used to go to with him and sitting in those places where they both used to sit together, that was what she kept doing, all the time. These activities relieved the hidden pain that she was feeling and which was not visible to the outside world.

She started feeling very low. She knew that her condition was worsening day by day. Looking at her phone every other minute for a call or message from him was beginning to make her feel embarrassed. She started requesting to God now for her better condition but God never comes to earth to save people. Rather, he sends some tools that give us direction. And in Anshu's life, that direction was Sakshi.

Anshu felt depressed and came back to her home with teary eyes. One more day of her life had passed with her just thinking about him. However, she was waiting for 2nd August, Ashu's birthday. She had decided to talk with him on that day obviously. How could she forget that day?

She had a feeling that something would happen then for sure. She remembered her birthday in October last year when she had been sad and suddenly the situation had changed to make her happy.

She was now feeling so depressed that she decided to talk to him. She checked his status on social networking tools in the night and saw that he was online. She felt sad. He had not sent her anything since the day they'd stopped talking, but he was busy with someone else in the night. She sent a message to him saying 'Hi', but didn't get any reply. After some time, she messaged him again saying; 'Hi Ashu'

Still she did not get any reply. She wanted to call him and dialed his number, but the line was busy. She dialed again after some time, but it was busy again. She took a deep breath and tried his number again many times over that night, but with the same result. Finally, his phone was switched off altogether.

She was annoyed now and felt very angry. Some days ago, she used to talk and chat with him the entire night, but now she called him twenty or thirty times in vain. She got no reply and then he'd switched his phone off. That meant he was ignoring her completely and enjoying his life.

She never expected such behavior from him. She'd thought that he was also in pain without her, but the reality it seemed was different.

Anshu was now feeling the pain of being ignored and that was very painful indeed. Even the next day she called him many times, but he did not pick up the phone. Even at night the line was busy, and then it was switched off. She prayed many times for reprieve, but God sometimes gives many things and sometimes nothing.

Anyway, as the next day was the 2nd of August, she sent out a message to him saying; 'Happy birthday and always be happy.'

And then sprawled on her bed.

Chapter 10

The next day, she slept until noon since last night had been full of tears and frustration as usual. After having some breakfast, she noticed that there were more than twenty missed calls on her mobile. All of them were from Sakshi and Manya. Manya had left home early that morning. Anshu called her.

'Where are you?' Manya asked.

'I was sleeping,' Anshu said.

'Its 1 pm!'

'Yeah I know. I slept very late last night.'

'Come to Sakshi's home immediately. I'm sending you the address.'

'But why?'

'Anshu, please don't ask questions. Just do whatever I'm asking you to do.'

'Okay I'm getting ready. Just send me address.'

'Get there as soon as possible.'

Manya messaged her the address. Anshu quickly got ready and left home. She reached the place at around 2.30 pm. 'What happened?' Anshu demanded. 'Why are both of you here and whose place is this?'

'Chill Anshu,' Sakshi said, 'Don't be aggressive now because you're going to get many more chances to be aggressive today.'

'What?' Anshu asked.

'Look Anshu,' Manya said, 'let me tell you everything in detail. As I already told you, I saw Ashu with someone else one day.'

'Yes, I remember. We've discussed it many times.'

'So from the day Sakshi approached him, they have both been frequently talking to each other and after one week they met and...'

Sakshi took over, saying; 'So when I met him the first time, he gave me a very innocent introduction to himself. He seemed like a person who was ready to give up everything for me. He told me that he's living here alone.'

'That's what he told me when we met the first time,' Anshu said.

'Exactly,' Sakshi said.

'And this was when you were both together,' Manya said, pointing a finger at Anshu.

'Yup,' Sakshi said. 'And then he insisted that I spend some time with him for a few days because he'd had a breakup with his girlfriend three months ago and was having some family issues as well. When I asked why he was disclosing his personal information to me, he said "Because I've been talking to you for the last few days and I'm feeling very comfortable with you". I was surprised by his statement.'

'Then they met again, the next day,' Manya said. 'And every day for the last two weeks.'

'Almost,' Sakshi said.

'Yeah, almost,' Manya said.

'And you know what he told me when I asked him why he broke up with his girlfriend?' Sakshi asked Anshu.

'What?' Anshu asked curiously.

'He told me that he was caring and a little possessive about her, but his girlfriend never liked that. He told me that he wanted to settle down with her, but his girlfriend just wanted to hang around with him.'

Anshu smiled a little, shaking her head. 'Did you ask for his girlfriend's name?'

'Yes. He gave me your name, Anshu.'

Anshu started laughing but then suddenly stopped and noticed that she was crying. She wiped away her tears and said; 'That's really good. Then what else did he tell about his damn girlfriend, Anshu?'

'I know this is painful Anshu, but you have to bear it with a brave heart.'

'No, I really want to hear everything and, believe me, I'm being brave.'

'Good. So he discussed everything about his family with me and then he asked me for a favor.'

'What favor?'

'He wanted me to spend some time with him over the next few days as he actually needs someone like me to help him overcome his problems in life,' Sakshi smiled.

Anshu was surprised. She had no option but to believe it because, during the initial days of their own relationship, he had said similar things to her too.

'So what plans do we have for today?' Anshu asked. 'I'm glad that you used the word "we",' Manya said.

'So as you know,' Sakshi said, 'today is his birthday. So he wanted me to spend some time with him and celebrate. And yesterday he also indicated that he wants to share something special with me today.'

'And what's that?'

'I don't know, but that's why we called you here. We need to catch him red-handed right now. That's what the plan is. Just wait here and watch what's going to happen. And after seeing everything, you can decide about him.'

Anshu said sadly; 'It is his first birthday since we met and I'd planned a lot for this day. How luck changes!'

'The change of luck and time can be positive or negative. The only difference is that positive change builds our life, and negative change destroys our life.'

Anshu asked; 'But Sakshi, tell me one thing. You have also spent some time with him. What is he like?'

'He's a very sweet boy who can win the heart of any girl,' Sakshi said. 'Seriously, those who present themselves as innocent and helpless are liked by everyone. They can win over any person without much effort. All they need to do is just talk and cry and people are in their pockets. Actually, this is the mistake of those who accept these kinds of people. I mean to say that I will never accept these types of people, because people who cry immediately when they meet someone are not actually innocent and depressed. Tears are precious things which should be shed in front of only very few people in life. Tears shed in front of many people have no value. Similarly, people who discuss their personal matters and issues with every second person at different places should not be entertained. They discuss these matters only to gain sympathy and attract people. They normally claim they are very kind-hearted people and easily convince everyone about it, but they do it just to gain sympathy and attention. I can bet on it that they never discuss their real issues. They just create false situations or manipulate their current situation so that it looks pathetic and then they show themselves to be helpless and poor so that people around them can care for them. An actual disturbed person will never discuss their issues with the people around them.'

'You are right,' Anshu said. 'These are simple things, simple to understand, but we never get them and then people make fools of us.'

'Exactly,' Sakshi said.

So three girls, one an innocent lover, the second a loving and caring sister and the third a smart person, all waited at the house for one boy. That's what Ashu always wanted, to enjoy his life with many girls, and that's what he was about to get.

Chapter 11

Sakshi got a call from Ashu. She didn't pick, but she got a message immediately after that. 'I'm there around your area. Please send me the address.'

Sakshi sent him the address.

Sakshi said to the other two; 'Look, I don't know how I'll handle this situation, but I will try. You both stay in the bedroom and lock it from inside. Manya, I'll dial your number and will keep my phone in my pocket so that you can listen to what we are saying. Got it?'

The doorbell rang.

Sakshi said; 'Go.'. Both Manya and Anshu went into the room. Sakshi dialed Manya's number. Manya picked up and Sakshi kept her phone in the pocket of her trousers. She opened the door and saw him standing in front. He entered the house with smile and asked; 'Do you wanna say anything?'

'What?'

'Are you sure you don't want to say anything?' he asked.

'No. Do you want to listen anything?' she smiled.

'Yes. I came here with a lot of thoughts in my mind, but my heart is broken now.' He made a sad face.

'Oh, poor Ashu. Okay, don't show me such a sad face and happy birthday.'

'Thank you. And by the way, where is my gift?'

'Wait Ashu, you'll get it soon. But please take a chill pill and have a seat.'

'Okay. I know a lot of girls don't care about boys normally. But we boys take care of things very well. See what I got for you.' He brought out a rose and gave it to her.

'Oh my God,' Sakshi said. 'Is there anything special about today for me?'

'No, but there is for me.'

'Then I should've given it to you. Why are you giving?' She took the rose. He came near her.

'No, Sakshi. You have already done a lot for me by staying in my life at my request when I was depressed. I mean who gives his or her time nowadays? Everybody is manipulative and fake.' 'Okay, tell me one thing seriously. Before this moment, with how many girls have you talked like this?'

'Are you thinking that I discuss my personal matters with everyone? No, not at all.'

'Then why me?'

'Look Sakshi, to be very frank, after talking to you on the phone, I realized that you are like me. Our way of thinking is the same and we even think in the same direction. So that's why I decided that I can share my personal feelings with you.'

He was showing the same kind of innocent behavior to Sakshi that he had showed to Anshu initially. Both Anshu and Manya were listening to everything. And if Sakshi had not been aware of this fake behavior, then she might have even fallen in love with him.

'Now what's the plan for today?' Ashu asked. 'Did you plan something for me?'

'Yes.'

'What?'

'Wait Ashu, don't be impatient. Okay, you told me you wanted to share something. What is it?'

'Nothing special sweetheart. I just wanted to spend some time with you today as I'm feeling very lonely nowadays. So I just wanted to be with you. Thank you very much for your company.'

'But why do you feel alone? I'm here with you.'

'That's the great part about today. I actually think of this as my birthday gift you know. That I'm spending today with a person who is similar to who I expect to have in my life.'

Anshu, in the other room, was listening to everything he was saying. She was feeling very bad. The same words he had used with her initially, he was now with another girl.

'Manya,' she said, 'this is it. I can't tolerate hearing any more. I want to slap him now.'

'Please Anshu,' Manya said. 'Wait till we get an indication from Sakshi.'

In the drawing room, Sakshi and Ashu were continuing their conversation. 'Okay,' Sakshi said, 'tell me, do you really think you are no more with your girlfriend? I mean it is personal, but if you want to share...'

'No, there's nothing personal between us now. You know everything about me. And as far as Anshu is concerned, we had a relation that was actually normal. We spent some fun time together. As you know, I'm a bit emotional so I engaged with her. But she was a different kind of person. She never looked into emotions seriously and just wanted to hang around with me for some time. And now she has gone out of my life.'

'Really? You mean it?'

'Yes. I'm not a strong person. That's why people come into my life, spend some time with, and then go away and leave me alone. But now I need a strong hand that can hold me and stay with me till the end.' He held her hand.

'Ashu,' Sakshi said, 'don't you think you are falling in relation as what I think we should always, rise in love and relation"

"Ok I am falling but can you hold my hand and help me to rise?"

'I'm not an easy thing to handle,' Sakshi said. 'Think twice before going around?'

'Look Sakshi, nowadays I only think about you and my heart only says one thing.'

'What?'

'Look, I don't know, but whenever I close my eyes, I see you in my dreams and when I open my eyes I wanna see you in front of my eyes at any cost all the time. When you are not with me, I feel you everywhere around me and when you insist on leaving me, I feel like I'm losing something very precious, and I suddenly start crying without you. People may call it love, obsession, madness, or anything else. I do not care what people say, but for me you are everything. I cannot leave you. In fact, I don't want to leave you because you are my identity now. And one can't leave his identity. I know many people were in love before I met you and a lot of people will fall in love after I die, but nobody is as lucky as I am because they do not have person like you in their life.'

This was the same dialogue he had given Anshu at Shimla. Anshu got completely disturbed when she heard this. She could not control her emotions and came out of the room immediately.

Sakshi immediately stood up, went over to her. Ashu was totally bewildered.

'Anshu,' Sakshi said, 'now it's your turn. How you will handle this is totally up to you. We are both out now.'

Anshu looked at Sakshi. Then she looked at him. He looked away.

'Happy birthday Ashu,' she said. He didn't reply. She said again; 'Ashu, I said happy birthday.' This time, she was much louder. And now he looked at her.

'What are you thinking about Ashu?' she asked. He now started smiling. He seemed to understand what was happening.

'Sakshi, what is this?' he asked. Sakshi did not reply.

'Ashu, damn it, what is this?' Anshu took a pillow and threw it at him.

'What?' he asked.

'Don't you understand what I'm asking?'

'Anshu, what is this drama?'

'Yes, that's what I'm asking you too. What is this drama?'

'I don't want to talk about this and I'm leaving.'

'Ashu, sit down and don't make me angry.'

'You are angry, Anshu.'

'Okay. Let's talk sensibly.' She took a long breath

'Not like this."

'Then shall we talk alone?'

'Yes.'

'Okay, let's go into the other room.'

'No issues,' Sakshi said, 'we'll go to another room.'

Sakshi and Manya left the room. Anshu said to him, quietly but with eyes filled with anger; 'Tell me what this is all about?'

'What is this baby?' Ashu said, his tone changed. 'I was not doing anything wrong. We are just friends.' He tried to hold her hand, but she did not allow him.

'Oh really? You are friends? Okay then, tell me why you were not picking up my calls or replying to my messages.'

'Look Anshu, I thought we broke up.'

'What are you talking about?' she asked loudly. 'You told me that day that we'll never meet again.'

'Don't put words in my mouth! I told you that we'll meet once you realized your mistakes and changed your behavior.'

'Same thing!'

'No, it is not the same thing. I was expecting you to change your behavior.'

'So it means you will leave me if I am bad.'

'No, I will give you some time alone to think about your bad behavior.'

'Look Anshu, to be very straightforward, I don't like you acting like you're my mom kind. It really irritates me.'

She lost control when he said that. A wave of anger took and she slapped his face angrily and started screaming. He lost his balance. Both Sakshi and Manya came out of the room.

He tried to stand up, but she pulled him by his collar and his shirt was ripped. He became angry.

'Anshu behave properly!' he said. 'What is this nonsense?'
'Ashu, you destroyed everything and now you're asking me to behave properly,' Anshu said and started weeping.

'Anshu, please don't cry,' Manya said.

'I'm not really crying,' Anshu said. But she was.

'I don't have any right to intervene,' Sakshi said, 'but I think you both should talk properly.'

'Sakshi, this is not good,' Ashu said.

'I know. But what you did and what you are doing isn't good either.'

'I trusted you.'

'What trust? You broke her trust. What trust are you talking about now?'

'I shared lot of personal things with you.'

'Oh come on Ashu. What did you share with me? The same things you share with every second girl you meet just to gain her confidence. And tell me, why me? You have such a sweet girlfriend who will do anything for you, who only thinks about you, talks about you, and cares for you. Tell me, why me? Just because you have spent enough time with her, you think you need a change. Ashu, please grow up. It's because of boys like you that girls start hating boys. Boys like you ruin the reputation of other boys too. You should be ashamed of what you did and what you are doing.'

'Have you forgotten all the time we spent together in the mountains?' Anshu asked him softly. 'You promised me that you'll never leave me.'

'You also enjoyed that time baby. The day and even the night… Didn't you?'

Anshu immediately got angry and spanked his face again. This time it was very hard.

'Manya, enough now,' Ashu said. 'I can't tolerate this anymore. And I'm telling you that if she does anything wrong again, then it won't be good for her. I'm warning you now.'

'What, are you fed up with me?' Anshu asked. 'I'm the person with whom you had dreams.' She pulled him towards her and spanked his face again.

Now Manya had to intervene. She took Anshu away from him and said; 'Now you will not do anything silly.'

'I'm not doing anything, it is all just happening. I love him and I can't hurt him.' She started crying very loudly.

'Please Anshu, don't cry.'

'I did so many things for him, always gave him every second of my life, thought only about him day and night and even gave him the love that any girl would think millions of times about before giving to any boy. I always kept my trust in him. I respected him a lot, and today he is saying he's fed up with me. He lost both my trust and respect. I was not with him just to enjoy my time, but to make him happy and because I believe that, in love, it becomes our responsibility to make our love happy. And look what he's saying now. That I was enjoying my time with him…'

She knelt down, covered her face with both of her hands, and started crying very loudly.

Manya said; 'Ashu, I think you should leave now.'

'No, he can't leave like this,' Anshu said. 'He has to answer for why he played with me like this. He started everything with me and he's now destroying our relation!'

'Look Anshu,' Ashu said, 'don't cry and I accept I wronged you. But I don't love you.'

'But why? If you don't love me then why did you come into my life and start everything? Anshu asked angrily and loudly, but still crying.

'Look, when we entered into this relation, I realized that we were not compatible with each other. I don't like people who are possessive and behave like instructors in life.'

'Ashu, you have broken my heart,' Anshu said. She was sobbing now.

'Look Anshu,' he said, 'I'm sorry. And please don't cry.'

'Sorry... That's it. That's all you have to say to me?' She held his hand, but he turned away. She felt terrible and continued looking at him. He ignored her.

'Ashu I love you so much,' she said. 'I was angry with you and gave you some space. But I never thought you'll leave like this. We were together for millions of seconds all day and night and felt each other everywhere. How could you be so cruel? If we are angry at each other and not talking, then does that mean we change the people whom we love? Please don't leave me because I love you straight from the heart and think about you every second. I can't even breathe without you. Please don't do this.'

'Sorry Anshu,' he said, 'this is not possible now.'

She was looking at him and, as he spoke, her expressions started changing. She again lost control, wanted to slap him, but she stopped her hand.

She screamed; 'Ashu, get out of here or else I will destroy myself!' And she fell down. Both Manya and Sakshi held her.

Manya screamed; 'Ashu, I am warning you now. Get out of here.'

He started leaving that place, but stopped when she called after him; 'Ashu, stop for a moment and listen to my last words.' He looked back.

Anshu said; 'Ashu, listen to me very carefully. I'm not accepting your apology now. I will accept it on the day you actually feel the same pain I am feeling today. On that day you will cry with the same pain I'm feeling now. What you need to do at that time is just close your eyes and say sorry. You will feel me around you then, I promise…'

'I was innocent and you have broken my heart. And whenever we break an innocent heart, we dirty our soul. I would request God to give you enough strength to wake up because now your time to wake up in life has begun. Now please get lost from here.'

Ashu smiled sarcastically and said; 'Anything else?' The way he saw it, what she was saying was just a filmy dialogue. He looked at her for a moment and then left the place. He did not look back.

She watched him go with tears in her eyes. When he was out of sight, she closed her eyes slowly and fell down completely.

She regained consciousness when Manya sprinkled some water on her face. 'Has he gone?' she asked.

'Yes.'

'Anshu,' Sakshi said, 'I know this is the not the right time, but I would expect you to behave like a mature person. You should look into the reality and the reality is that he was a betrayer, a bad person, a hound. And you are lucky that you understood that soon.'

'I am not lucky, Sakshi,' Anshu said. 'Lucky people get the shining of the moon. But look at my bad luck! I didn't even get a broken star from the skies. That's the story of my life.'

'It's not like that Anshu,' Manya said as she caressed her face.

'Ok, let's go home now,' Anshu said to Manya. 'I want to get some rest.'

Manya wanted to say something, but Sakshi stopped her. And then they all went back to Anshu's home.

Now things were clear for both Ashu and Anshu. The relation was over.

All the plans that they had made together were over, as were the promises that they'd made to each other.

Ashu was relaxed about it. He wanted this breakup. He'd got lot of hard hits from Anshu, but he was still relaxed because now he was free to enjoy other relations. Anshu was a different kind of girl. He had never expected a girl like her. He'd always wanted a girl more like himself.

On the other side though, he was the first boy in Anshu's life. And she had decided to settle down with him. Now he was gone. How was she going to come out of this stage? That was the big question.

Chapter 12

Ashu came out of the building. This was the worst day of his life. He had completely forgotten that today was his birthday. Suddenly, he got a message from one of his friends; 'Hey dude, what's the plan for today?'

He read the message and switched off his phone without replying. He sat in his car and bowed his head. He never ever expected this would happen. He was actually thinking about his plans with Sakshi which were ruined now. He always played around girls softly but smartly, and now he'd become a victim himself.

Suddenly, he started laughing. He said aloud; 'Oh God, what is this? I never expected this and that to on my birthday. You have given me such a great gift. Thank you very much. I will remember it always. But did I do anything wrong? I think when two persons meet and enjoy their time together, they both enjoy it. So why regret? When two persons are physically intimate, they both enjoy it. So why feel pain and cry then? We should move ahead and look for another person. Life goes on. When we were together, we enjoyed. And now when things are not compatible, that is it. It's over. That is life. That's how it should be.'

He looked at his reflection in the glass of the window. He suddenly realized he was talking to himself. It was the time he was ever doing it and he was shocked.

'Come on Ashu man, what are you doing? You are not this kind of person. Do whatever you want to do. Now the best part is that Anshu's chapter is closed. She was nothing but a pain. She's gone now. To get something in life we have to lose something. So don't regret and move ahead.'

He looked up and felt better. Then he decided to go to his room and take some rest. He was feeling low still though. His face had got lot of hard hits from Anshu. He had never ever been slapped before, not even by his family, as he was the only son of his parents. Anshu was the first person in his life who'd spanked his face.

He reached his house at around 7 pm. His roommate was out of town, so nobody was there to disturb him. He switched on the TV to watch something, but could not find anything to watch at this time. He wanted to go out and have a drink or something, but then he decided against it. He sat on the chair and started watching something on TV and, very soon, he fell asleep.

When he opened his eyes, it was morning. He got ready quickly, but felt confused. *Where to go man? College friends? Hmmm… Nope. Nightclub friends? Maybe, but I will call them in the evening. What to do now?*

Suddenly he thought about Anshu. Normally, at this point of time, he used to call her as she was the only person who would be available all the time. Now he could not even talk to her after. Suddenly, he thought to check his social networking tools to see his friend list. He saw many people who were online.

Whom should I contact? Ankit? No he is boring. Reema? No, again a boring girl. Prem? No, he always talks about his girlfriend; not tolerable. Rakesh? He is interesting.

He sent a message to him saying; 'Hi,', but got no reply.

Suddenly, he got a message from Riya, one of the girls who had a crush on him. He never paid her much attention in college because of Anshu, but right now anything would do.

'Hi Riya,' Ashu said.

'Hey… What doing?☺' she replied

'Nothing special. You?'

'Same here.'

He noticed that her status was ☹ (feeling sad). So he asked her; 'Why so sad?'

'Nothing,' she replied

'You can tell me.'

'Nothing. But feeling sad.'

'But why?'

'Just had a fight with my friend.'

'Okay. We could meet today if you are feeling sad and have a discussion.'

'Are you sure?'

'Yes.' Ashu gave her the location and said; 'I'll pick you up.'

Yesterday he'd had a break up with his girlfriend and today he was going to help a person who was sad because she'd had a fight with her friend. He could not save his own relation but he was trying to save others.

Anyway, they met in the evening and went to a restaurant. They had a good time, ate dinner together. After dinner he asked her; 'Can we go for a long drive?'

'How long?' Riya smiled.

'Well it depends how long you can take it,' he said, looking into her eyes.

'Okay,' she said. And they went for a long drive.

'Okay tell me what your issue is,' he said. 'You told me that you had a fight with your friend…'

'Yeah, nothing special. It's a routine fight between us, but I feel sad when I fight with anyone I like.'

'But then why are you still friends with a person whom you fight with on a regular basis? You should leave such a friend?'

'Why should I leave a person who is really dear to me? We fight on a regular basis, but that doesn't make me want to leave my friend. Look, we meet many people in life, but we connect with only a few of them. Very few of them in fact. We talk to many people, spend time with a lot of people, but we lack one thing and that is connection. We connect only with those who care for us, who look into our problems sincerely, feel our pain as they do their own, who really stay with us through our worst times, who want to see us at our worst and who tolerate us at our worst. So if we find such a person in life, then why leave just because we have fights? We fight because we have differences of opinion but for that small reason we shouldn't abandon our relation. That is stupidity. Got it?'

He nodded. Nowadays, he seemed to only be meeting people who were lecturing him about relationships. Even Riya who liked him very much in college was giving him a lecture. He'd thought to spend some quality time with her. But now he regretted his decision.

I'm not in a good mood. I brought her here with me to set my mood right, but look what I'm getting instead.

As he was thinking this, Riya asked; 'Ashu, how is Anshu?'

'I don't know.'

'What? Did you have a fight with her?'

'I don't know,' he said, annoyed. 'I mean to say that she is out of station.'

'Where did she go?'

'She went to her hometown for a few days. But you tell me what's going on in your life these days?'

'Nothing special. Just the routine work. But I hope you're enjoying your life with Anshu.'

He started feeling very fed up now. Very soon, he turned back home. On the way, he listened to all her boring lectures. He dropped her home and while he was driving back to his house, he started laughing.

Ashu what's happening with you man? Did you really love Anshu? It is frustrating now and you have to do something to get away from this word "Anshu." You don't believe in love. It is not difficult for you. You can do it because you are a strong person and you can come out of any situation. It's not impossible; nothing in this world is impossible. What you need to do is engage yourself somewhere else. Need to find some other girl who is compatible with you. Anshu was not compatible with you. She was a mom, not a girlfriend. And you need a girlfriend who can help you relax as Anshu used to be some months ago. You can find better than her and one who is compatible with you.

Anyway, as the days progressed, he talked and chatted with lots of people but he got no peace of mind as everyone was asking him about Anshu. The last few days had been like a year for him. One day he was sitting at home in a bad mood. He was thinking how his life had changed after Anshu. He started looking for options again. He thought about one of his good friends, Andy, who was a party animal. He called him. 'Hey dude, how are you?'

'Oh man,' Andy said. 'Long time. What's up?'

'Nothing. Just wasting time.'

'Why, what happened? You are not the sort of person, who wastes his life,' Andy laughed.

'Just tired dude. Anyway, what's going on with you? Parties and all?'

'Oh yeah. In full flow. Me and parties are like a brother and sister who can't live without each other.' He laughed again.

'Then what are you doing tomorrow? Meeting with your sister? If so, then would you let me meet your sister?'

'Why not man? You can meet my sister anytime and enjoy.'

'So send me the details.'

'There is a party going on in the outskirts of Delhi tomorrow. Would you like to join?'

'Sure. Send me the details.'

Andy sent him the address details. He took a long breath then and sprawled on his bed.

'That's the spirit man,' he said to himself. 'That's my real Ashu. Now you are behaving like Ashu. People know you very well. What are you doing, getting so tense over one girl? There are millions of girls out there and they are all waiting for you.'

The next morning, he was fine. He woke up at 11 am and got ready for college. He'd not gone there for many days, and decided now to go just to be with friends for a change. He was worried that he might see Anshu at college, and about what would happen if he did. But then he thought: *why worry? And now I can face any situation as I've seen worst of her already...*

He met with all his friends in college. But everyone was asking him only one question: 'Where is Anshu?' Because nobody had seen Anshu for many days and she had not been online on any social networking tool for a while. He had no answers and told everyone that she was out of station.

He checked her status. It showed that she'd been offline for the last few days. Whether she'd changed her number or was not well, he didn't know. Then he met with one of his good friends, Amit, who was aware of their fight.

'What happened?' Amit asked.

'Nothing,' Ashu said. 'Just came today to meet you guys.'

'You are looking upset. Is everything fine? And I hope that all your issues with Anshu are resolved?'

'No. It's all over now.'

Amit was astonished. 'No man, don't say that.'

'No. I'm telling you the truth.'

'What happened?'

'Just compatibility issues.'

'It took you guys one year to figure out you had compatibility issues? I thought you couples were forever.'

'No. Nothing last forever in life.'

'I agree. But what exactly happened?'

Ashu told him everything – except his own mistakes.

'But why did she do all this?' Amit asked. 'I thought she was crazy about you.'

'She started spying on me and sent one of her friends to keep an eye on me.'

'So she caught you flirting with her friend?" He asked curiously

'No. Her friend asked me to spend some time with her. She wanted to share some of her problems with me and that was it. Anshu walked in in between and created a scene.'

'That's not good,' Amit said. 'She should have had faith in you. So you guys are no more together. But are you worrying about her now? She did wrong and she should realize it. She has already beaten you for no reason. I think all her love was bullshit. You should not contact her now and mind your own business because you are correct and you know it. So just go ahead and concentrate on your current relations and friends.'

Anyway, he got ready as soon as he reached home. He was supposed to meet Andy at a point near the place where the party was happening. He was looking forward to the evening. He had decided to start over again now that he had left Anshu. He had removed a scene-creating person from his life. And who cared what the depth of his relation with that person had been?

Chapter 13

In the evening, at around 7:30 pm, Ashu left for the party. It was a rainy evening. The weather was giving an excitement to the heart of those who had their love ones with them and the same were giving sadness to those who were sitting far away from their love ones or who were carrying distances in their heart even if they were physically close.

But don't offend climate for making people sad and admire it for making people happy. The problem is, fate for those who believe in luck or attitude for those who are practical and do not believe in luck.

He called Andy as soon as he reached the place because he could not find him. Andy came over to him in a bit. Ashu noticed a very gorgeous and sexy girl with Andy.

'You are late man,' Ashu said to Andy.

Andy laughed. 'No problem brother. Good things come late in life, but when they come, they give unforgettable pleasure.'

They both laughed and Andy gave him a very tight hug. However the girl standing besides Andy was not laughing. She was searching for something on her mobile. Ashu said to Andy; 'By the way, I just saw a beautiful face here, but it seems she doesn't have any interest in giving us a smile.'

The girl ignored him completely.

'Shut up you hound,' Andy said. 'She's my fiancée and her name is Tanya.'

'Oh, I am sorry,' Ashu said. 'You know me Andy. I'm just like that.'

'I know you brother,' Andy said. 'Don't be sorry.'

Ashu introduced himself to her saying; 'Hi, my name is Ashu and I am still a bachelor.'

Tanya simply said 'Hello'. She then turned to Andy and said; 'I'm going inside, so can we please walk, if you don't mind?'

'Why not sweetheart,' Andy said. 'Anything you say.'

Now they entered the party. She was wearing an outfit that was very revealing, but she behaved as if she came from a conservative background. She was behaving like a girl who only looks at and talks to her husband or fiancée. Suddenly, Ashu realized that she was the fiancée of Andy who was a very dangerous person. He had connections with the police and with all those people who can create a nuisance in our society with all their power and money.

When he entered the house, Ashu felt amazed by the atmosphere inside. It was rocking everywhere. People were having fun all around. The party seemed to have everything that was needed for one to have fun. Everything seemed good, especially the girls. He started thinking about what to do first. This was the first time in a long time that he was coming to a party.

He decided to have a small drink to start the evening with and to get into the flow of the party.

Suddenly, he felt someone touched his back. It was Andy. 'Hey man, what's up? Enjoying or not?'

'Not started yet,' Ashu replied.

'You used to be a different kind of person. I feel now that you are waiting for something to happen. Come on man. Leave everything behind and go ahead in life. By the way, you used to have a girlfriend no? What was her name? I forgot...'

'Anshu.'

'Yes, Anshu. You showed me her picture.' 'Yeah.'

'Yep. So now you've left her yes?' 'Yeah, I left her.'

'So why are you so sad about it? It's good to have change in life. I believe in that whether its underwear or girlfriends, we should change them after some time. Otherwise it just starts itching and gives pain. Just use them and leave them,' Andy said loudly.

'Yeah man,' Ashu said. 'That's a good policy. I admire it.' 'I know you've shown me her pictures. And probably she came for the New Year party. She was hot. I never told you this when she was your girlfriend, but now I can say it. She was hot and pretty. I believe you have tasted and tested her completely.'

Ashu did not say anything, just smiled. Andy said; 'I know you are bastard as far as these things are concerned and that's why I love you like my brother.' He took Ashu in his arms.

'Okay,' Ashu said, 'leave this topic and tell me how you got this beautiful lady, Tanya?'

'You liked her.'

'No man, just asking.'

'I know she is a thing to be looked at, stared at actually.'

'But she is your fiancée.'

'I know, but I can't prevent people from looking at her. She is smart and sexy and I enjoy it.' Andy winked.

'Great,' Ashu said. 'But where is she?'

'She must be around somewhere, but you stay away from her because she is very hard to handle.'

Ashu smiled and said; 'Don't worry, I'll take care. But now I really want to enjoy the party.'

They stepped on to the dance floor. There was passion all around. Ashu was drinking, and he had no idea how much he drank. It seemed there was no tomorrow. He started dancing with a girl. His hands were soon on her back. They got very close to each other and suddenly the girl kissed his lips, looked at him, and then started walking away. It seemed she was giving him a sign to follow her.

He understood the signals and started following her. She took him to a corner near the changing room. She looked at him passionately as if she wanted him to hold her in his arms. He did not waste any time in wrapping his arms around her body and then they started kissing each other passionately. They were kissing each other with full lust and passion.

Suddenly he heard a loud voice say; 'Ashuuuu' – and the event that had happened back at Sakshi's place suddenly came back to him. He felt somebody spanked his face hard. He immediately drew away from the strange girl, but she pulled him back to her and said; 'Come to me you smarty.' She started kissing him again, but he forcefully withdrew from her.

She got angry and said; 'Lay off you bastard.'

He turned around angrily and stepped up to hit her, but then suddenly he heard a voice say; 'Hey, stop all this nonsense.'

He turned back and saw Tanya. He controlled his anger. Meanwhile that strange girl sneaked away. He lost control, but regained his balance immediately. Tanya started laughing.

'What happened?' Ashu asked. 'Why are you laughing?'

'Nothing,' Tanya said. But she was still laughing. 'Was the kiss not going well?'

'What?'

'I saw you both kissing each other passionately. What happened? Why did you stop and leave her?'

'It's not good to spy on others having a scene.'

'Really?'

'Of course.'

'If you think so, then why were you creating them with your girlfriend at a place that is open to everyone?'

'She's not my girlfriend.'

'Okay, so then she must be your wife or fiancée.'

'No.'

'No? She is not your girlfriend nor are you going to marry her. Are you a male prostitute?'

'What?' Ashu looked angry now.

She smiled and immediately left that place. He was surprised by what Tanya had called him; a male prostitute. Why she called him that, he did not know. But he wasn't the kind to leave questions unanswered. He went to the party room again to see her. He tried to find her. Suddenly someone spanked him from behind. He turned back. It was Andy.

'What's going on buddy?' he asked.

'Nothing,' Ashu said.

'But your eyes suggest that you're looking for someone.'

'No, just chilling out.' Ashu looked around and noticed Tanya coming in their direction.

'Hey sweetheart,' Andy said. 'What are you doing? Are you comfortable?'

'Yes,' Tanya said.

Ashu was continuously observing her. In front of Andy, she was like a person who didn't have a tongue in her mouth. She was now showing the kind of behavior that she displayed only when she talked to Andy.

Now Ashu became more curious about her. But he did not get any chance that night to interact with her. The party ended at around 2 am and he left the place immediately. But in the car, he was continuously thinking about her. Suddenly he remembered that she was Andy's fiancée but then he thought: *Lay off Andy, I'll do what I want to do. And Tanya has given me enough to think about*"

He was now thinking about how to contact her. Even her mobile number would do. But how to get it? That was the one thought that haunted him all night.

Chapter 14

The next day, he started scratching his head as soon as he woke up. He had to get her contact details. But how? He thought a lot about it and then decided to call Andy.

'Hey Ashu,' Andy said. 'How are you brother?'

'I'm fine. Where are you?'

'I'm about to go out to take care of some urgent business.'

'Seems you're still hung-over from last night.'

'What? No way, I'm totally fine'

'It doesn't seem so, judging by your voice.'

'No way.'

'Okay, let me check … Do you have any idea when we left the party last night?'

'Of course. We left at around 2 am.'

'And what was the color of my shirt?' Ashu laughed.

'I don't know. I don't like boys.'

'Okay, what was the color of Tanya's clothes? Do you remember?'

'Yeah of course. It was blue.'

'Okay great. Now I know you are clean. So you're both going together?'

'No, she's not with me.'

'Why, I thought you live together all the time and that you've left her in the house all alone.'

'Yeah we live together, but this morning she went to meet her office friends I believe" Apparently she'd gone to some shopping mall.

'How do you know she is there? She could be anywhere now. And by the way, I know you don't believe in girls. She might flirt with someone else.'

'No way. You know me, Ashu. I don't let go easily. And if she does that then I'll kill both of them. You know I can do it easily.'

'I know man. You are very dangerous.'

'Since birth,' Andy said. And they both started laughing. 'Okay brother,' Ashu said. 'I've to go somewhere urgently. See you.'

'Sure man, enjoy,' Andy said. He disconnected the phone. Ashu looked at the phone and said; 'Andy, you are a jerk in more ways than one. Anyone can steal your property if you're going to throw information around like this.'

He did not think twice. He left the house and went to meet her at the shopping mall. He parked the car in the basement and pushed the lift button. He was surprised to see her leaving the lift, but her eyes were lowered and she started walking away. He called her; 'Excuse me ma'am.' She turned back. 'I think I know you.'

She didn't reply and started walking away again. 'Tanya, what happened?' he asked. Now she stopped walking and looked back.

'What? She asked.

'I'm calling you, so why are you walking away?'

'Because you are asking fake questions.'

'What?'

'You know me and my name but you're still saying "I think I know you". I know very well that I'm a thing to be remembered forever.'

'I'm sorry. I was just having fun. Really sorry.' They were quiet for a moment. 'But two things you should remember. One, you are correct. No one can forget you. Second, you are not a thing.'

She curiously asked him; 'Who are you and why you are here?'

'My name is Ashu and I –'

She cut him off; 'I know you are single so don't say it again.'

'Okay. And I'm here to ask you to answer a question that you left unanswered last night.'

'Which is?'

'You look mature and also sound intelligent. You should remember.'

'Well I don't.'

'Okay, I'll give you thirty minutes to remember what the question was.'

'Until then?'

'I won't mind having coffee with you.'

'Look Ashu,' she said after a thoughtful pause, 'I don't mind, but your friend might.'

'Oh come on Tanya, we are not going on a date. We just met here. So what is the issue?'

'Okay then,' she said.

'After you,' Ashu smiled.

He got his chance. This was what he wanted. They were sitting in the coffee shop. 'So what did you shop for today?'

'Nothing. This isn't what we were supposed to discuss.'

'Tell me one thing,' Ashu said. 'Why are you so straightforward?' He asked the question aggressively and she liked that.

'Okay, I'm sorry,' she said. 'But did you come here to ask just this? Wait, how did you even find me?'

He told her the entire story. She was surprised. 'Do you know Andy might kill you for this?'

'Tell me, who is Andy to you? Do you want to marry him?'

'He is my fiancé.'

'That is not the answer to my question. I'm asking if you want to marry him.'

'What is this nonsense? A fiancé is a person a girl plans to marry.'

'Exactly. *Plans* to marry. Only planning. Not marrying.'

'What is the difference?'

'I'm trying to say that sometimes a fiancé may be an infliction.' Ashu smiled. But she turned away.'

'Tell me what question I left unanswered last night,' she asked.

'That is not the answer to my question.'

She started laughing. 'What is your type? I am not getting you at all. Okay, tell me what that question is?'

'Why did you call me a male prostitute last night?'

'Does it bother you?'

'What bothers me is how one can be a male prostitute if he kisses an unknown girl.'

'Why were you kissing her? Okay, tell me, have you ever spent time with a girl who sells her body for money?'

He was surprised by her question. She went on; 'Tell me, have you ever been with any such girls? They do everything, you know. But not for love. They satisfy the lust of some civilized people just for money, so that they can live life happily with their families. They become things which we can use for our pleasure and to slake our lust. However, when the same girl does the same things for love, she becomes a girlfriend or a wife. We do not accept these kinds of women in our society though they are an integral part of our society. That is why I called you a male prostitute when I saw you kissing an unknown girl.'

'I think the difference between the two is love.'

'Exactly. That's why love and relationships have been proved to be sacred in our society – because it cleans the image of sex. When we use sex in a relationship, then it becomes sacred. When we do it without love, then it becomes a crime that is infamous, reprehensible, and defamed everywhere.'

Ashu smiled and bowed his head.

'Don't smile. I'm serious.'

'I'm just trying to understand what exactly your point is.'

Again he'd met a person who liked to give lectures, but this time he was enjoying it. After all, he had just met her and in the initial stages of any relation, we enjoy everything the other person says even if it is bullshit.

'Tanya, tell me something,' Ashu said. 'Where and when did you meet Andy?'

'In Mumbai.'

'What were you doing there?'

'Why do you need to know that?'

'I am wondering what I was doing when you met with him.' He said, clearly flirting.

'Well I met him two months ago. So what exactly were you doing then?'

'Nothing. Just having fun with my friends.'

'Any special friend?'

'No. Just a normal friend circle.'

'You don't look like a person who wastes his time. Guys like you normally waste your time and money on some special friends without any reason.'

'I think you have a lot to say about some special kinds of boys. Would you like to share with me?'

'I think you don't want to meet me tomorrow. That's why you're asking everything today.'

'No, actually I was giving you heads up for tomorrow's discussion.' They both smiled.

Tanya asked; 'Ashu, tell me what type of person you are.'

'Well, I'm an interesting type of person.'

'Really?'

'Yes. Try me.'

They looked into each other's eyes for a long moment. Then she said; 'I like boys who can poetize.' She smiled

'I can do that,' Ashu replied immediately.

'Okay then, sing me a poem.'

'Let me try.'

He was about to start, but she interrupted him saying; 'But it shouldn't be filmy.' She raised a finger at him.

'This is not fair. You should understand the feelings.'

'What feelings? You should know how to create things. You guys always copy dialogues and songs from movies.'

'So what?'

'If you can create false situations as you did today to know where I was, then why can't you create real things? Let me tell you one thing. The day you start doing it from the heart, you will stop copying stuff and create something of your own. That is called creativity.'

'One day I will perhaps. But for now can I copy?' She was about to say something, but then suddenly she noticed her phone. There were many missed calls from Andy.

'Oh shit!' she groaned. 'He's going to kill me.'

'What happened? Tell him you were busy.'

'No Ashu. You don't know him. He will kill me. I'm leaving.' He saw fear in her eyes. Her face that had been gleaming one minute ago now became dull.

'Shall I drop you somewhere?' Ashu offered.

'No I'll manage. Bye.'

'See you,' he said. She did not reply. 'I said see you,' he repeated. He held her arm.

'Ashu,' Tanya said, 'don't even try to call or message me. I'll do it, if possible.' She immediately left that place.

He started thinking about her behavior. He was rather surprised to see her reaction to Andy's missed calls. On his way back home, he thought to himself:

What's wrong here? It was just a few calls that she didn't pick. She was behaving as if she had committed some crime. I think Andy behaves the same way with her that Anshu used to with me. I hope she will be fine. God help her.

He kept thinking about her and, when he reached home, he started waiting for her call. Now she had his number as they'd both exchanged numbers during their talk. However, he did not get anything from her side for next two hours. He then picked up his phone to call her.

What will happen if I call her? Will she mind it or not? Oh come on Ashu, why are you thinking so much? If there's any issue, I can take care of it...

He gave her a missed call, sent a message to her saying; 'It's me Ashu', and then went to sleep.

Chapter 15

He checked his phone as soon as he woke up to see if there were any missed calls or messages from Tanya. But there was nothing. He started thinking about last day when she'd left him with a fear of Andy in her eyes. He thought a lot about it and then decided to call her. If anything bad happened, he would take care of it and if it didn't then he wouldn't care.

He was starting to care about her. This is actually a very beautiful phase in life wherein we are enamored by the beauty, nature, and attitude of someone. This feeling is sacred even if it exists inside a person like Ashu whose mind was in the control of the devil.

In Ashu's case, when he met Tanya, he was mesmerized by her beauty and face. However, when he noticed the fear in her eyes, he became worried. And now he decided to call her and protect her if anything bad had happened to her.

He called her many times but again with no success. Then after some time he sent a message to her saying; 'Call me now', but did not get any reply. After five minutes, he again sent her a message saying; 'Call me. Otherwise I'm calling Andy and asking about you.'

She replied to that. "Ashu, please stop this nonsense,' Tanya said.

'Where are you?' Ashu asked. 'You promised to meet me today but you didn't even send a single message. This is bad.'

'I didn't make any promise and you are disturbing me now.'

'I'm coming to meet Andy and will see you there.'

'Okay come. I'll complain about you to him.'

'Please do it now. Do you really think I won't come if you complain?'

She did not reply for some time. He sent a message again: 'Tell me, you really think so?

'Okay. Come. And be prepared for the worst.'

She sent him her address. He'd again got what he wanted, a chance to see her. Along with a challenge. He'd always liked challenges in life and she'd given him one. It seemed she wanted him to come otherwise she could have easily say no for the address detail

He did not waste a single second. He changed and left the house. They were both at a hotel. He reached the place in half an hour, parked his car, and immediately went to the lobby – which was near the swimming pool. He noticed Andy relaxing after a swim. He went to him.

'Hey Andy,' he said. 'What's up man? What are you doing here?'

'Oh man, Ashu; nice to see your face,' Andy said. 'What are you doing here?'

'Nothing. Just came to meet a friend.'

'Boy or girl?'

'What do you think? I'm not of an age or mood to meet boys.' And they both started laughing. 'Are you alone here or is someone with you?' Ashu asked.

'No man. She's with me.' He gestured backwards. And Ashu was amazed to see her coming towards them in a swimsuit. She came and sat near Andy. She looked at Ashu and smiled sweetly.

'Oh hi. You are Ashu right?' She pretended as if she was meeting him for the first time after the party.

'Yes, I think so. But I'll double-check with my parents and see if they've given me the same name or not.'

'Excuse me guys,' Andy said. 'But I need to take this call.' He saw that his phone was ringing. Tanya started to wrap a towel around herself.

'Why are you wearing this? It's not needed with me.'

'Shut up,' she said.

'I asked why are you wearing this?' he repeated. 'It's not needed with me.'

'What's wrong with you? Why do you want me to not wear it?'

'Because I'm not looking at your body. I'm just looking into your eyes, your glittering beautiful eyes.' She looked at him, surprised, and shook her head.

'By the way,' Ashu said. 'Is he complaining to the police about me or arranging for some guns to shoot me?'

'Who are you? And do you really think it is so easy to be a cool dude in any situation?'

'Nope. Not easy, but we can try as much as we can. By the way, why didn't you pick up your phone? I was calling you.'

'I was busy with Andy.'

'Were you guys having sex?'

She looked at him angrily and made to leave, but he held her arm.

'Okay, I'm sorry.'

'Ashu, you should –'

He cut her off. 'Okay, I'm just kidding baby. Leave it. What's wrong with you? Why do you become aggressive all the time? I want to see the Tanya of yesterday evening. A sweetheart.'

'Don't call me sweetheart.'

'But you are a sweetheart.'

'Why did you come here? Don't you feel scared of him?'

'Why fear when you are my dear?' He laughed.

'It is not funny Ashu,' she said. 'Andy might blow you.'

'He can't because I know you won't let him blow me.'

'Look Ashu, I'm gonna marry him very soon.'

'Really? But it doesn't seem to be happening?'

'What do you mean?'

'I am saying that it seems he wants to marry you. But you are staying with him as a slave. I could use an ugly word too.'

'What do you mean?'

'You're afraid of him and you think that if you don't marry him he'll kill you.'

'It's not like that. And I'm going now.'

'You can go. In fact you should go but at least turn back once.'

She turned back, looked at him for a while, and then left that place. He looked up at the skies and started laughing.

'I am giving lectures to her. What's happening to me? I'm behaving like someone has walked out of my life.'

He did not wait for Andy and simply sent him a message that saying; 'I have to go urgently', and left that place. He switched his phone off as soon as he reached home and slept.

He woke up at around 8 pm in the evening and checked his phone for any call or message from her. There was nothing. He felt neither happy nor sad. He said to himself; 'No worries, Ashu dear. It's party time now.'

He changed his clothes and called one of his friends, but this friend declined to join. He did not care. He started his car and reached a disco club to enjoy the evening.

He was amazed by the atmosphere inside the disco. It was rocking. He drained a large glass of wine in one sip. He then jumped onto the floor and started dancing with some unknown people. But he left the floor after sometime, took a chair, and amused himself by just watching people.

Everyone was dancing with wild energy. They were doing everything; dancing, laughing, and screaming – all for no reason. Ashu looked at everyone in the club. He thought: *It's rocking but one thing I'm not sure of is why they are all dancing. Are they happy or not? I think we dance if there is a special occasion happening in our lives. People here are laughing and screaming, but why? Are they happy or has something happened in their life today?*

'No,' he heard a loud voice say.

It could be heard over the loud music. Ashu turned left and was surprised to see a person sitting with him. This person was looking exactly like him. But this reflection of his was looking like a gentleman with decent white cloths.

'No,' this person went on. 'They are dancing because everybody here is dancing and because it's praxis to dance here at this place and nothing else. They do not have any other reasons. If they actually had any happiness to share with anyone, then they would have been with their families and loved ones. But they are here wasting their money and energy.

'They are laughing because everybody here is laughing. But actually they are wasting their smiles. Some of them are smiling to hide their actual feelings. They are sad inside; I can bet on it. After this party they are going to cry alone. They came here to ignore their problems for some time and see who is dancing with them.'

Ashu looked to his right side and was shocked to see himself dancing in between them. He watched himself dancing wildly and passionately. He was screaming and laughing loudly. Now Ashu was standing between two of his own reflections. He again gazed at the decent-looking one. This reflection asked; 'Tell me brother, why are you dancing and laughing? What you have done in your life? Have you achieved anything that is remarkable? How many girls you've been with in your life and what do you think about them? What did you do with Anshu? What will do with Tanya? If she is actually having a problem, then you know what to do, you know the path. For that you need to look into your own past because the past contains the answers to all the questions that we face in the present and will face in the future. Good or bad doesn't matter and only foolish people say that the past gives us disappointments only. We need to broaden our vision, and the correct vision comes from taking the right step. And remember one thing: when faced with a dilemma, stop walking and wait for the right time to come.'

Ashu was looking into the eyes of his decent-looking reflection. The eyes of it were glittering with confidence while the eyes of the real Ashu were full of frustration and confusion.

'Who are you?' he asked his reflection.

'I'm nothing but who you can be in future if you want to be and the Ashu on the dance floor is who you are now. You can also continue to be that Ashu. The decision is yours. You can choose either of us. We both live inside you. Normally people call me the Angel and the one on the dance floor the Devil.'

The reflection started walking away. The volume of the music increased again. Ashu turned back towards the dance floor and saw his other refection, the smart but indecent looking one, dancing and screaming like there was no tomorrow.

Then he suddenly thought about the lecture that Anshu used to give him. About life throwing difficulties at us and how, in the end, the choice is up to us, how we can choose what is right or what is easy...

He looked at the Ashu dancing wildly and then at the other Ashu who was going away from him. Suddenly the decent-looking Ashu stopped and turned back. He winked once at him.

Ashu was continuously staring at his two reflections.

He had to choose between them.

He looked down, thought, looked up again, turned to his left, looked at the decent-looking Ashu, and smiled. It seemed he had picked the Angel over the Devil.

He closed his eyes, smiled, and when he opened his eyes again, he saw Andy in front of him, looking angry. Andy took a gun out of his pocket, screamed, and put a bullet in his heart. People around cried out with terror as Ashu fell down and closed his eyes.

Suddenly, he opened his eyes – and found himself on his bed.

Oh man. Shit. It was a dream… What's happening to me? What was that? I saw myself in three different forms and then Andy shot me down. What is this nonsense?

He went to the washroom and threw some water on his face. There were lines of tension on his forehead.

Anshu or Tanya?

He was confused. He'd never been so tense before. He checked his phone and noticed that there were three messages from Tanya: 'Where are you?', 'Are you busy? Please message me once you are free', and 'Okay. Good night.'

He read all her messages, but did not react. He could not even smile. He looked at his phone, thinking. It was 3 am. He thought for a while and then replied to her saying; 'Sorry, was tired so slept. Just woke up.'

'What happened?' she messaged back. 'I thought you'd died ☺'

'☺' Ashu replied.

'Sorry. I never meant that ☹'

'I know.'

'All well?'

'Yes, of course. Just restless.'

'Okay. Can we meet tomorrow at the same place we met two days ago?'

'Sure. Will catch you there at around 4 pm.'

'Okay. Good night.'

Ashu immediately switched off his phone, went to bed, and started thinking about his life. He closed his eyes and fell into an uneasy sleep.

Chapter 16

He woke up late the next morning but finished whatever he had to quickly because he was supposed to meet her at 4 pm. He called her as soon as he reached the place. She did not pick up the phone, but she messaged him saying that she would reach in ten minutes.

He waited for her at the coffee shop. She joined him after a while.

'How are you?' he asked her.

'Great. Did you get enough rest last night?'

'Yes. I'm glad you remembered me last night,' he smiled.

'Ashu, you are still flirting with me.'

'Not at all. That's your problem Tanya. You don't take me seriously.'

'I am now.'

'Really?'

'Yep.'

'So if you wanted to meet me, I guess you have something to say.'

She did not answer at once. 'Yes,' she said after a thoughtful silence. 'I wanted to ask you something. Yesterday, you came to meet me. Even after I warned you not to come.'

'I think I've already answered this question yesterday.'

'Yes. But why? I'm not your girlfriend. I am Andy's fiancée and he is very possessive about me. You know this.'

'Yeah I do. So what?'

'So there's nothing serious here?'

'Nope.'

'Ashu.'

'What Ashu?' She stared at him. 'Okay,' he said after a small pause. 'Why are you thinking so much about all this then? Do you care about me?'

'This is not funny Ashu. And why are you taking such an interest in my life? Please stay away from me.'

'Tanya, look into my eyes and tell me if you really mean that.' 'Look Ashu,' Tanya sighed. 'I'm very disturbed nowadays and I don't want anyone to be part of it.'

'Exactly!' Ashu said. 'That's what I'm trying to find out. Because I saw a glimpse of fear in your eyes that day when Andy called you and you didn't pick up. I'm not able to understand what you're doing. If two people really want to be with each other, then there is no place for fear. You can fight, you might abuse to some extent, show some attitude, show some aggression, but fear should not be a part of it. Why do you feel afraid of him? Did you commit some sin that cannot be forgiven? Even in that case, you should have the guts to be able to say to your partner; "I did a mistake, forgive me. It's my right to be forgiven by you because we love each other."'

They both were quiet for a moment. 'Look Ashu,' Tanya said. 'I've read somewhere that there are a lot of things in life which we cannot express or explain, but that doesn't mean they do not exist in our life. And that is true.'

'Look Tanya, everything in life is explainable and expressible if we want to discuss it. But if we close the doors and don't discuss, then your code is true. Are you saying that whatever is happening to you is not explainable?'

'Yes.'

'Then I'm sorry to say it, but you just don't want to discuss it. It is okay with me if you don't want to discuss it, but don't say your issues are not explainable.'

'It's not like that,' Tanya said. 'But –'

'Look Tanya,' Ashu said. 'I know you aren't feeling good. And one thing I can say is that you don't seem to be happy with what's happening around you. If you do not want to get married, then don't. As per my understanding, marriage is a relation wherein we give our whole lives to someone and in return take his or her life. So if we don't want to get married, then why do it? Why waste a relationship just because we have some pressure on us?'

'So what should I do?' she asked aggressively.

'Tell him you don't want to get married. That's it.'

'Look Ashu, I belong to a poor family. And I met Andy when he came to our state on some business trip. We interacted there and then I came with him here because he helped my family to some extent.'

'Are you saying your family sold you for money?'

'It's not like that. I also wanted to marry him. That's why I came here. But after reaching here, I came to know his true personality. He spends time with many girls. Sometimes he behaves like a wild animal. But I'm really not in a position to do anything.'

'You can do one thing. Leave him.'

'It's not so easy. In fact it's impossible.'

'No it isn't. And it is easy. Just come out of the house at night.'

'And where do I go? It's not so easy. You don't know him. He can do anything and reach anywhere.'

'But we can do a lot of things also I'm sure.'

'What? Are you saying you'll help me get out of his place?'

'No. I'm saying I'll come with you and help make things easier for you.'

'No Ashu. It's sweet of you. But I can't do it.'

'But why? Why can't you do it? Don't worry about me. Let me tell you this; when two people are together and working for a cause or purpose, then they can make anything happen.'

'But why would you do this for me?'

'Look Tanya, when I saw you for the first time, I lusted for you. I thought I would eat you from top to bottom because you were looking so sexy and gorgeous. One thing is certain though now. I don't love you. I might like you, but I don't love you, even though I'm not sure what love is. In fact, I don't believe in these things. For me, if we are spending time together, making each other happy, then it means we have something special between us. But when being with each other is a source of pain and tension, then better to walk out of the relationship. We should always look for better options, and, if we really want it, we can get better options in life. People who give us pain should be left immediately, irrespective of the relation.'

'What we are about to do will give you pain in the future.'

'No, it will give us adventure and excitement. Believe me.'

'It's not about the adventure Ashu. It is about Andy who is very possessive of me and could be dangerous. Why are you taking such a risk for me and what about your studies?'

'I don't know. But I think we should do it. I can manage my life.'

She seemed reluctant, but since he was pressing her, she asked for some time to think about it.

'Okay think about it,' he told her. 'But decide soon. Deferring a negative event will only increase its adverse impact.'

It was almost nighttime when they finally left that place. He sent her a message later: 'Decide when you want to leave. I'm waiting.'

She replied with a "☺".

For the next three or four days, everything was normal. He chatted with her through texts but got no response with regards to his proposal.

One day, while he was watching TV in the evening, he got a call from Andy. He was surprised and didn't pick up. Then he got a message from Andy saying; 'Call me as soon as you see this message.' He didn't reply, but his mind began to race.

What happened? Why is he calling? Did he come to know about our plan? No way. It's only between me and her...

Then he wondered if she was okay. Andy was dangerous and could do anything. He called him back.

'Hey Ashu,' Andy said. 'How are you brother?'

'I am fine man,' Andy said. 'How come you remembered me?'

'I just wanted to know if you'd like to come home tonight. We're having a party tonight.'

'It is night, Andy.'

'But our nights start after 11 pm only,' Andy laughed.

Andy's behavior seemed suspicious, but since Tanya was there, Ashu decided that he had to go. He said to Andy; 'I'm coming. See you there.'

'Great. See you there.'

He got there at 10.30 pm. It seemed that Andy was waiting for him. He took Ashu to the basement of his house where many people were gathered.

'It looks like a real party,' Ashu said. 'Any occasion?'

'A special one,' Andy replied. 'Today I'm going to announce my wedding to Tanya, so I wanted to have a small get-together with all my friends and brothers.'

Ashu was shocked, but he concealed it. 'Congratulations, Andy my brother,' he said and gave Andy a big tight hug.

'Thanks bro,' Andy grinned.

'Where is the sweet lady?' Ashu asked.

'She's coming.'

After five minutes, Tanya came. She was looking awesome. Andy announced; 'My dear friends, meet my to-be wife Tanya. We will be getting married next week so if anybody has any objections, then let me know.'

Everybody started laughing loudly. Ashu included. She was staring at him. He went to congratulate her. Now the party was really starting. But he was only looking at Tanya, as she was at him.

Andy came up to him. 'How she is looking?'

'Who?'

'Ashu, I've been observing you for the last fifteen minutes. You've been continuously staring at my sweet wife.'

'To-be wife,' Ashu said. They both smiled.

'You were a bastard from the time I met you,' Andy said. "And that's why I like you.'

'Since birth man,' Ashu grinned. But he sensed that something was wrong. He kept his courage though. He was at Andy's party and behaving. He wasn't scared of anything. They both turned to look at Tanya.

'You know Ashu,' Andy said, 'the thing I like about her most is that innocent face and cute behavior.'

'Really?'

'Yep. But you know what I think about girls. They can't be decent. They'll be with us while they are happy and then ditch us suddenly. I love Tanya and want to be with her. She makes me feel good at night when she sleeps with me and even during the day. But I still think she is with someone else even while she is with me in the night. I don't know why I feel this. But I do know I can kill anyone for her.'

'You should kill anybody who comes between you and her," Ashu said.

Andy suddenly started laughing. "This is why I like you. You think like me.'

'No, I think a little differently. I don't believe in violence and forced relations. If a girl doesn't want to be with me, then I don't force her because she will not give me happiness.' Ashu smiled a little, looking Andy right in the eye.

'But we are both bastards.'

'Yes we are. At least ethically we are.'

'But what about that girl, Anshu, who you left some weeks ago? I thought you would continue with her for a while longer. She was a cutie. Very beautiful…'

He started getting angry, but he controlled himself quickly. 'Leave her,' he said. 'I don't remember the girls from my past. And she was not meant for me. She was the kind who treated her partner like God.'

'She was a fool then.'

'Whatever. That was her perception of life and relationships.'

'It seems you were serious about her.'

'It's not like that. But I think I need to go now. I'm very tired.'

'Sure. But you really are sounding different today.'

Ashu immediately left that place and came out of the party house. But as he neared his car, Tanya called him. She was standing in a corner. It looked like she'd been waiting for him. 'What were you guys talking about?' she asked.

'You didn't tell me you guys were engaged,' Ashu said.

'I didn't even know myself.'

'Really?'

'Yes.'

'I was waiting for your call, but I got one from Andy instead.'

'He's going to marry me next week, Ashu. It is not going to be easy for me to leave now. He has announced the engagement in front of many people. So…'

'So what?'

'Ashu, it is dangerous and you know that. It seems to me that he knows about our meetings.'

'That's good,' he said. She looked at him, surprised, but could not say anything. He went on; 'Tanya, decide now whether you want to do it or not. I'm not a person who asks again and again.'

'Then why are you asking me again and again?'

'I'm asking you to decide.'

They looked at each other. Tanya said; 'It may be life-ruining.'

'When do you want to do it?'

'It might spoil your career too.'

'You need to be very careful until we leave. But after that I'll take care of everything.'

'Ashu,' Tanya said. She stroked his cheek as if imploring him not to do it.

'Let's do it,' Ashu said. He nodded his head once to express his willingness to go through with the plan.

She sighed after a while; 'Okay. Let's do it. But mind you I'm not as confident as you are.'

'No problem. If one person is confident and the other just follows, everything will be fine.'

'I have to leave now,' Tanya sighed. 'Give me tomorrow to prepare.'

'You have tonight and tomorrow. I'll message you the plan very soon. Remember, it won't matter whether we do it tomorrow or the day after. It will still create the same impact. So we'll do it as early as possible. Got it?'

She gave him a smile and nodded. 'I'll rely on what you send me and act accordingly.'

'Don't worry,' Ashu said. 'I won't let you down. Trust me and don't sleep tonight till you get a message from me.'

He had made a similar promise to one of the girls in his life some months ago, while they were making love and spending time together, but he'd broken that promise very soon and now he was making another promise to Tanya.

"Trust me" and "Believe me" and "I won't let you down" are words which we tell many people in life, but when the time comes to prove ourselves we actually come to know how tough it is to act as we promised. Therefore we should be very careful while saying these valuable words.

Right now, Ashu did not even know how he was going to keep his promises to Tanya. He was just excited, enthusiastic, and wanted to look like a hero in front of a girl. His confidence and courage were admirable though.

One thing was for sure though. This journey was going to change their lives. For better or for worse, nobody could say yet.

Chapter 17

He got home at around 2 am. On his way home, he was continuously thinking. He had to be very careful while planning for tomorrow. He remembered what she'd said about Andy not being an easy man to handle.

But what would Andy do if they left tonight?

He thought for the next one hour and then started typing a message to Tanya. It went like this:

'Today, at 5 am in the morning, that's one hour from now, you'll be out of Andy's home. I will pick you up from the back of house. Don't take anything with you. We'll manage everything later. Don't carry anything. Read this message five times and then delete it. Take care.'

He thought about it for two minutes and then pressed the send button.

He looked up and then closed his eyes. He said to himself; 'Are you sure, Ashu? You are doing it because you are a different kind of person. You have never taken up responsibility for anything in your life until now. And you are asking a girl to leave her fiancé's house. Why? Do you love her or do you like her?'

He got up from his chair and said to himself; 'What's going on? Is it just that I don't want to be here for some time? And because she doesn't want to marry Andy and doesn't want to stay with him? So we're both on the same page; what's wrong in it then? And Andy can't do anything. If he calls the police, well, Tanya is a mature adult so no issues. And if he tries to use any of his criminal contacts he still can do nothing. She'll be gone and won't be coming back.'

He checked his phone and saw that she'd replied saying; 'Okay. And I have deleted the message.'

He geared up, took a bath, changed his clothes and made some coffee. He was going to have to drive and drive fast, away from this place. He checked if he had everything; his wallet, all his cards, driving license, pollution, and insurance. He sent a message to his roommate saying he was going to his hometown for a few days.

He got a message from Tanya. 'How much money should I take with me?' she asked.

'As much as you can. I am leaving now so get ready.'

He left his house at 4.30 am. Before starting his car he looked up and said; 'This time I am doing it for somebody else and not for myself. So please be with me.'

Tanya was waiting for him. He opened the door of his car and she got inside. She was wearing blue jeans with a black top. She was also carrying a handbag.

'Wow, you are looking gorgeous,' Ashu said. 'I've never seen you in this outfit.'

'Let's go. We can talk later,' Tanya said.

'As you say.' He started the car and drove to the highway. "Highway" is a word that means different things to different people. It is the one thing that leads to change in people's life, but it never changes its own aim, which is to connect.

It connects one state to another, one culture to another and one linguistic region to another. People change their ways of living, dressing and talking as the highway progresses. Sometimes and somewhere, the highway itself changes its size and look, but it doesn't change its aim. While humans normally change as they go through life. We cannot describe what a highway means to us in one go as it carries so many stories.

Ashu had come here the last time with Anshu, and in different state of mind. They had both wanted to achieve something in their life, and that they had done. Now, once again, he was coming here – and this time with a different person. They both had their own dilemmas.

Ashu's dilemma was Anshu and Tanya's dilemma was Andy.

As their car came on to the highway, sun started rising. He played some music that was fitting for this lovely morning.

She seemed relaxed. He thought she was asleep, but noticed that her eyelashes were moving. He wanted to talk, but did not want to disturb her. He drove fast and soon he saw Tanya opening her eyes and start looking outside. All the villages, farmlands, and crops on the outskirts of Delhi were looking very beautiful in the morning light.

She closed her eyes as the wind blew on her beautiful face. 'What happened? Why are you so quiet?' he asked her.

'Nothing,' Tanya said quietly.

He changed the song and played some fast numbers of his choice.

'Ashu, please play some songs that are light and heart touching.'

'Why? These songs are touching my heart. I like them.'

'But I don't. They are touching my mind, not my heart. So please change them.'

'Okay, as you say.' He changed the music and played some soft music for her

'Tell me if you don't like anything. I'll change it,' he said.

'I will. You concentrate on driving.' She closed her eyes again

He did as she instructed. After a while she said; 'I'm getting hungry. Please get me some food.'

'Okay let me find a good restaurant.'

'Anything will be nice in this weather. I also wanna have some tea. Do you get it?'

'Okay,' Ashu said. There were lots of restaurants passing them by.

'Ashu what are you doing?' Tanya demanded. 'You are leaving everything behind. I'm hungry!'

'I understand that. But those restaurants are on the other side of the road. The traffic is too heavy. I can't cut across to them.'

'You should have thought about that earlier. You should have gone on to the left side of the road like all those other cars right at the start. You didn't even bring a bottle of water with you.'

'Okay. Give me two minutes and I'll try to get to that side of the road. The traffic is moving very fast.'

'Do you always keep making excuses for your mistakes, Ashu?'

'Do you think I'm making fake excuses?'

'Yeah I think so.'

'Tanya, you wanna fight?'

'No, I wanna eat something. And if you don't get me something to eat now, then I'll eat you.'

Finally, he got them to a restaurant where they could park the car and eat some food.

'What do you want to eat?' he asked her.

'Anything but fast.

He ordered a *Puree choley* and tea for them both. After finishing breakfast, they started enjoying the tea.

Ashu said jokingly; 'You ate like you hadn't seen food in years.'

'Shut up.'

He started teasing her about how much she'd eaten. She was now staring at him angrily 'Ashu, do you really mean what you are saying?'

'Yes baby,' he said.

'Okay. I'm leaving this place.'

'Think about it. What will you do if your buddy Andy catches you? And I have the car.'

'Who says so? I am using the car. I've got the keys. It's you who'd better worry about Andy catching you.' She walked away. He checked his pocket but could not find the keys.

'Hey, Tanya!' he cried. 'Stop! When did you steal the keys?'

'It's an art and you won't get it, you duffer boy,' she said.

He ran very fast and finally caught her. He held her tightly and tried to take his keys back. People at the restaurant were staring at them.

'Leave me you jerk,' Tanya hissed.

'I will once I get my keys back.'

Finally, he managed to get his key from her. She spanked his arm a few times and then they both started laughing. Their chemistry was fantastic.

They got to the car, but then Ashu suddenly realized that he'd left his mobile back at the table. He immediately went back to get it. As he neared the table, his expression changed drastically.

Actually, this was the same place where, some months ago, he'd come with Anshu. It was not by chance that he'd stopped his car at this restaurant. It was intentional.

He stopped, closed his eyes, and thought for a moment about the time he'd spent here with Anshu. Suddenly, the vibrations of his phone made him snap out of his thoughts. Tanya was calling him. He was in such a good mood, but now thoughts of Anshu had made him sad again. He picked Tanya's call.

'Where are you?' Tanya asked.

'Coming. Two minutes,' he said.

When he rejoined her, she said to him; 'Ashu you were right. This was the first time in a long time that I really felt hungry and ate properly.'

'I understand,' Ashu smiled.

'No, you really can't understand what I felt today. We learn only though experiences, and the last few months with Andy have taught me a lot. When I was with Andy. I used to eat just to survive. I used to laugh just to make people around think that I was feeling happy. Now I've decided that will never go back to that place. I'd rather die than go back there.'

She held his hand and said; 'Ashu, thank you for a getting me out of that hell.'

"Really but don't be as these are formal words and we shouldn't use them all the time".

'Yes, you are right. But if I can't be thankful to you, then what can I do?'

'Nothing for now. If there is anything, I'll tell you. Okay, tell me how you're feeling now.'

She closed her eyes and took a long breath. 'On top of the world. Fine and light.'

'Good. Okay, its 9 am now. You should switch off your phone.'

'Why?'

'Look Tanya, I think we should start being a little cautious now because this is a very critical step we've taken. We have crossed some limits. You were engaged to Andy and now you've run away without telling him. We both know that he is a different kind of person. He'll try to catch you. And by keeping your phone on, you are giving him an invitation to catch us.'

'Okay. I'll do it. But what's our plan now?'

'Plan?'

'Yes. We've taken such a big step. You said you'll manage after I agreed to it.'

'Yes, I'll manage. But I have no plan…'

'Ashu, please tell me you're joking,' Tanya said slowly.

'I'm serious, Tanya.'

'Ashu, are you crazy? Okay, where are we going now at least?'

'I don't know.'

'Oh please Ashu. Don't say that again.'

'Look Tanya, I asked you to switch off your phone. That's the entire plan we have now.'

'And then?'

'Then we'll see.' He turned away.

'I don't believe this,' Tanya said. 'We've taken the biggest risk of our lives and we have no plan. Wow. Great. Fantastic.'

'Thank you sweetheart.'

That annoyed her. 'Oh shut up Ashu,' she yelled. 'And I don't believe I have taken such a big step,'

'Oh really? Just five minute ago you were enjoying yourself.'

'Forget about that. I'm just asking you how we could take such a big step without a plan. You said you'll manage.'"

'I will manage.'

'How?' she demanded. 'Actually, I think you cannot do anything. The only things you can do are things that don't matter like dancing and fighting on the road. This is bullshit.'

'What?'

'Yes!' I trusted you and –'

'And I suggest you keep trusting me. If not, we're both going to be in big trouble indeed.'

She was about to snap back, but just then her phone rang. It was Andy. She did not pick it up. She then switched the phone off as Ashu had told her to. Then they both got into the car and sped away from that place.

113

<h1 style="text-align:center">Chapter 18</h1>

Neither of them spoke. Andy had called. And that meant he knew that she was not in the house. And still they had no plan. They were now running away from their problems, not knowing where they were going or how far they would have to go. Tanya kept her fingers crossed. She was angry. He played some music, but she switched it off.

'What happened?' he asked. She didn't reply. He asked again; 'What happened baby? Why are you so angry and nervous?'

'Ashu, could you please stop bullshitting?'

'What bullshit? Did I ask him to call you? You were in such a good mood. And now you're being mean just because he called you.'

Suddenly, his own phone rang. He got a shock when he saw that it was Andy who was calling him. He did not pick up the phone. 'Does he know you are with me?'

She shook her head silently and closed her eyes He got another call from Andy. He thought for a while. 'I am picking it up.'

'Do you know what you're doing?' Tanya asked.

He did not reply. He picked up the phone and put it on speaker. 'Hi Andy,' he said.

'Hey Ashu. Where are you?'

'I'm at home.'

'Oh really? Are you sure?'

'Yes Andy.'

'Ashu, I told you last night that I can do anything for her, that I can kill anybody. I don't know what I'll do to her for this betrayal when I catch both of you, but I'll surely kill you man. I am warning you. Leave that hound girl right now and I'll let you go. But if you stay with her, then I'll kill you first.' Andy hung up with that.

They were both terrified. He started driving, but not as fast as before. She was looking at him. He was looking very worried.

'Please turn around and go back to Delhi.'

'What?'

'Turn around.'

'Look –'

'Ashu, turn the car around or else I'll jump out.' He stopped the car. 'Please Ashu,' Tanya said. 'Turn around. This won't work.' He thought for a while and then did as she asked.

He started driving back to Delhi, watching her out of the corner of his eye. Suddenly a car hit their car. Their car lost balance. She screamed loudly. He pressed the brake pedal. He managed to stop by the side of the road. They both were stunned. He suddenly saw that the car that had hit them was coming back in their direction.

'Start the car and drive!' Tanya screamed. 'I think its Andy!'

But the car stopped and an old man got out. Ashu also got out. The old man said to him; 'Watch the way you are driving.

It is the highway here and you are driving as if you are on a local road. It is dangerous. Are you okay?'

'Yes we are okay,' Ashu said. 'And I'm sorry.'

'Okay, drive safely,' the old man said. And then he left that place.

Ashu came back into the car. 'He was just asking if we were all right. Nothing more.'

He noticed that her eyes were wet and, when he held her face in his hands, she started crying loudly. He consoled her. She stopped crying after two or three minutes. He wanted to say something, but stopped himself. He started driving again. He kept going straight for the next half an hour. But then, suddenly, he took a U-turn just before reaching the border.

'What are you doing?' Tanya shrieked.

He stopped the car, thought for a while, picked up his phone, and dialed a number. He put the phone on speaker. It was Andy.

'Hey Andy, what's up man? Ashu here.'

'Yes Ashu,' Andy said. 'Glad to hear your voice brother.'

'Don't be and listen to me carefully. I'm taking her out of here, Andy. I don't know where. I have no plans. You are my good friend, but this is about her. She does not want to be with you and this is more than enough reason for me to take her away from you. If you understand, then it will be good for you. But if you don't get it then it is your problem not mines. You can catch me and kill me if you want. In fact, please kill me because if you do not kill me then I'll kill you. See you man.'

He hung up. He now seemed confident, positive, and decisive.

'What is this nonsense, damn it?' Tanya demanded. He did not reply. She asked the same question again, pulling his arm now. But this time he reacted, and reacted very loudly.

'Shut up! Shut up, shut up, shut up! And don't say another word for the next half hour! You got that?'

He started driving very fast now. She was shocked by his behavior, but he was so angry that she didn't dare say anything more. He had never behaved in such a way with any girl before. Actually, in all his life, he had never ever been serious with a girl. He spent his time with many girls, but only while he was comfortable. All his love and dedication went into gutter after that. That was why he used to be such a cool dude.

He drove for about an hour. Then he stopped. 'My head hurts. I want to have some tea. Do you?'

'No I don't.'

'Okay, as you wish,' Ashu said. 'Let me know if you want anything.'

She thought he would apologize for his behavior, but he did not seem about to do that now. After a while, she too went into the restaurant. She could not find him. Then she saw him coming out of the washroom.

'What happened?' he asked. 'Are you okay?'

'Yes,' she said.

'Would you like to have something?'

'What are you having?'

'Tea.'

'Get two then,' she smiled. She went to a table and took a chair, sat down. He came up with two cups of tea.

They both started drinking the tea quietly. He seemed lost in his thoughts. She suddenly nudged his leg with her right foot. He looked underneath the table and then stared at her. She smiled at him; 'I think you are hungry. Please eat something.'

'No I'm not.'

'You are. I can see it in your eyes, from the way you are staring at me...' She wanted to say more, but she thought better of it.

'Let's go Tanya,' he said. They both got inside the car.

'Can I ask you something?' Tanya said.

'What?'

'Do we know where we're going?'

'No. We need to make a plan.'

'We don't have a plan yet?'

'No. I told you this already. I'm sorry. But we'll have one soon.'

'So what are you thinking about now?'

Somebody knocked on the glass. It was a cop. He asked them not to sit in the car. If they need to talk, they could sit in the restaurant, but not in the car. Ashu immediately started his car up, but the cop stopped him again.

'What are you carrying in the car?' the cop asked.

'Nothing,' Ashu said. 'Why?'

'Show me the back seat,' the cop said. Ashu got out and opened the rear door. He was shocked. A lot of money was spread out all over the back seat. The cop asked them to come with him to the police station. Ashu took the police officer to one side and they had a very long discussion. It seemed that Ashu was trying to convince him about something. He finally showed the cop something from his wallet and shook hands with the cop. He got back inside the car.

Before he could ask, Tanya said; 'Okay, let me tell you. Since we were running away from the city, I thought we might require some money to survive. So I took some money with me.'

'How much is this?' Ashu asked.

'I think it is two lakhs or might be three I didn't notice. I picked it from Andy's bag in hurry. He was drunk and unconscious.'

'What nonsense is this Tanya? You should have told me!'

'I was going to, but things were becoming chaotic. Sorry Ashu.'

He shook his head, frustrated, and started driving.

He was in the worst position possible. He was taking away with him a girl who was the fiancée of one of the most dangerous businesspersons in Delhi – and who had already warned him that he was going to kill him – and now he was also carrying a lot of cash in his car, which was illegal.

'Why are you so quiet?' Tanya asked him.

He didn't reply.

'Ashu, stop the car,' Tanya said.

He ignored her.

'Stop the car,' she said again. 'We need to talk.'

'Keep quiet for some time,' he snapped.

'No.'

'Why can't you shut up?'

'What's your problem?'

'My problem is you and your attitude!'

'What? My attitude?'

'Yes.'

'Let's get out of this car and talk.'

'Okay,' Ashu said.

'Let's' He got out of the car aggressively, as did she. Now they both started fighting on the highway. Their voices were almost drowned out by the noise of the traffic.

'Okay, tell me what's wrong with me now,' Tanya said.

'Tanya, I am actually not in a position to argue right now,'

Ashu said. He turned away. She pulled at his arm. He tried to get away.

'What do you think of yourself? You have brought me here and now you're showing attitude. Are you trying to show off? Trying to pretend you're doing something for me?'

'Stop this nonsense,' Ashu snapped. 'I can't tolerate it anymore. I have a headache now. How difficult it is for you to understand that we are in deep trouble? You always talk about sensibility. Look how sensible you are. You are blaming me. You're saying that I am trying to show off. I am just trying to be with you. Isn't that enough for you? You want more. Well if you want more, then you need to tell me what you want. I will do it for you, but don't use such language with me. Behave properly, or at least try to.

'A girl should be sensible like Anshu. She was younger than you, but as far as sensibility and responsibility was concerned, you can't touch her. She always protected me from bad things. She taught me the things I'm telling you. She was a girl, but she always came up to save me and guided me in life. Made me choose the correct path. But I never listened to her and I finally lost her because I treated her the way you're treating me.'

Tanya was standing like a statue and was shocked to see some tears coming out of his eyes. His eyes were wet, but he was still getting angry. He turned his head away and wiped his eyes. She was still just standing there. He took a water bottle from the back seat and washed his mouth and eyes.

Then he turned to her and said; 'Tanya, without any further argument, please get inside the car.' She did what he said. Night was falling now. He started driving again.

They drove in silence, but after a while he started feeling bad. 'I'm sorry Tanya. I lost my temper. I'm really sorry.'

'Who is Anshu?'

'Nobody.'

'If a person is a nobody, then they can't make us cry. Especially not in your case.'

'In my case?'

'You don't seem like the sort who cries at all. I'm surprised a girl could make you cry.'

'My head was hurting,' he mumbled. 'That's all…'

'Look at me,' Tanya said. 'I'm such an innocent-looking girl and you are getting angry at me for no reason.' She gave him a sweet innocent smile to change his mood.

'Can we play some music if you don't mind?' she asked. He switched on the music and smiled. The radio channel was playing some light music. Things were looking better now. He lowered the volume of the music and said; 'I think we should stay here for tonight. It's been a tiring day. And we need some rest. What do you say?'

Tanya agreed. They started looking out for some place to spend the night in and found one soon. They took two rooms for the night. He knew the place they were at was Panchkula that was near to two beautiful places Chandigarh and Shimla. They ordered coffee as soon as they entered the room. The weather was good. They were close to the mountains.

'What is this place? It looks beautiful.'

'Yes, it is indeed a very beautiful place. It is near Chandigarh and Shimla.'

'Near Shimla? I've never been there. I want to see it. Can we go there tonight?'

'Not tonight. It's hilly and not safe to drive to at night.'

'Okay,' she smiled. 'You can take me there tomorrow morning. I'll manage tonight.'

'Great. But we can go to Chandigarh tonight for dinner if you want.'

'Okay. I'd like that.' She was excited. They drank their coffee and relaxed for half an hour. Then they went to Chandigarh for dinner.

Chapter 19

Chandigarh – a very beautiful place with big flat roads that were cleaner than those of Delhi. Tanya was enjoying driving on these roads.

'How are you feeling?' Ashu asked her.

'Good. Fantastic actually.'

Before going for dinner, they stopped at a clothes shop. They decided to buy some clothes because they did not have anything other than what they were wearing. She insisted on paying for all the stuff they purchased. They came out of the shop and then found a restaurant to have dinner in. They were enjoying every single moment in this beautiful city though they were in trouble. After dinner, they went to a local shopping mall and had ice-cream. Then they sat down on the steps of that shopping mall.

Ashu said; 'We'll go back to the hotel now. It is almost 11 pm.'

'No,' Tanya said.

'Huh?'

'If you're asking me then the answer is no, But if you're telling me we have to go back, then all right.' She turned her face away, pretending to sulk.

'Okay,' Ashu said. 'We'll go back whenever you want. In fact, let's play a game.'

'What game?'

'We won't go back until we've tired ourselves out completely. What do you say?'

'Not a bad idea,' she smiled.

He decided to change his behavior completely. He had to be mature now. Before, Anshu used to be the mature one. But now it was his turn. He looked at her eating her ice-cream.

I'm not sure what I'm doing, I'm not sure where I will be or what I'll do tomorrow, but right now I'm thinking only about her. I've never before felt like this in my life, never had tears in my eyes, but today I had them. I don't know how to behave in these circumstances because I've never done anything beyond my limits for anybody. I've done that for her and I have no choice now but to keep doing it. If she can think and act beyond her limits for me, then why can't I for her?

He said quietly to himself, or perhaps to God; 'I'm sorry I hurt you that day, Anshu. People like me are not made for you and I don't deserve you. But look at me now. I am again using you for my benefit. I'm going to do what you would have done for me. I'm sorry again, and I hope you know it. You promised that you'll know when I truly felt sorry...'

He heard Tanya said then; 'Why are you laughing?'

'Nothing.'

'You use that word a lot. If we smile or cry, then there is definitely something that's causing it. And I want to know what that something is.'

'Look Anshu,' Ashu said. 'You have lot of things to say. How do you manage to say all these things?'

'I am Tanya, not Anshu. You just called me Anshu.'

'Oh! I'm so sorry. I meant Tanya –'

'Stop. Now tell me who this Anshu is, I want to know. I'm serious.'

He didn't know what to say. 'She was just a friend.'

'Really? Are you sure?'

'Yeah. So do you like this city?'

'Ashu, don't change the topic and tell me who Anshu is.'

Just then, two cops came to them and asked them to go home as it was almost midnight. They both stood up and started walking towards the parking area.

'People don't want to see other people happy,' Tanya grumbled.

Ashu shrugged. 'It's a rule. We have to follow it. It's for our safety.'

She held his arm and said; 'Tell me honestly now, have you ever followed a rule in your life?'

'No. But just because we didn't do something doesn't mean we'll never do it. We can start anything, any time.'

'You've changed since we started this journey,' Tanya observed. 'You're more serious now. I never imagined you could be like this. I'm impressed.'

He smiled and they both got inside the car. 'By the way, I forgot to ask what you said to that cop who caught us in the restaurant.'

'Well, I created a story,' Ashu grinned. 'I told him that you are my girlfriend and that your parents did not want us to get married. And that you left your house for me and took this money with you so that we could spend some days together.'

She started laughing. 'Really? You really told him that?'

'Yep,' Ashu said. They got back to the hotel in a good mood. She asked him to come and be with her in her room until she fell asleep.

'Now what the plan is for tomorrow. Are we going to Shimla?' she asked.

He took a long breath. 'Well, we have to spend some time – one or two days – coming up with a proper plan. So yes, we can go to mountains. It will be a good fun.'

They talked for a while longer. Soon, she fell asleep on the bed and he slept in the chair, still sitting up.

They slept until 10 am the next morning. The hotel staff called them for breakfast. She ordered breakfast and saw him sleeping on the chair. She started smiling. She knew that he had started taking care of her now.

She called him very softly, but there was no response. Then she went near him and touched his face. He opened his eyes.

'What happened?' he asked.

'Nothing,' Tanya said. 'It's morning. Wake up, go to your room, and get ready for breakfast. Come on, hurry up.'

Over breakfast, they discussed their plan. 'So,' she asked, 'what do we have planned for today? I mean where do we go?'

'You should be ashamed,' Ashu said, having some fun with her. 'We are not here for a picnic.'

'Well, since you don't have a plan, we might as well have some fun in the meantime.'

He said to her teasingly; 'The last two days, you've been expecting me to come up with some plan. We're both here. We're both in trouble. Why don't you come up with a plan? Or at least give me an idea?'

They were actually having fun together now.

'Okay,' Tanya said finally. 'Here's what we'll do. You'll come up with the plan. I'll look into it and tell you whether it's any good or not. All right?'

'Okay, but finish your breakfast quickly. We need to check out fast. It's not a good idea for us to be here or anywhere else for too long.'

Now they had a plan to go to Shimla, but they had no plans on how to solve their problems. They were both reluctant to even think about it. They were enjoying each other's company – which would have been a good thing in any situation apart from the one they were in now.

They went out immediately after breakfast. It was a nice scene outside. On one side, the mountains were stretched out in a chain. It looked lovely.

'It looks awesome!' Tanya exclaimed. 'Perfect setting for a picture! Please take a picture of me Ashu.'

'No,' he said. 'Let's go now. We can take a lot of pictures in Shimla.'

'Ashu, how rude you are,' Tanya said. 'You are denying me again.' She spanked him playfully. She was happy because they were now going to the place she'd always wanted to go to.

She looked at the chain of mountains that stretched out in front of her with a hope of reaching them soon. He was smiling and felt the wind on his face. Both his hands were in his pockets. His expression was dreamy. His eyes glittered every time she smiled.

Was the same story that had played out a few months ago going to repeat itself? They both seemed very sensitive towards each other. Their chemistry was fantastic. He had started behaving in a very mature way, but she on the other hand seemed childish and possessive.

People who have different mindsets and behavioral patterns are sometimes more compatible with each other than people who are very similar. People with similar natures end up getting annoyed with each other very easily.

Ashu and Tanya seemed compatible with each other. In fact, they seemed to be completing each other.

Tanya pointed at the highest peak of the mountains. 'How long will it take for us to reach there?'

'We have to die to reach there because that point is not reachable,' Ashu told her before he started driving

As they entered the valleys of the mountains, they saw a lot of cops going in the same direction and lots of people standing on the road. It looked like they were discussing something serious.

'I think something has happened here,' Tanya said.

'Let me see,' Ashu said. She wanted to go with him, but he told her not to. He started inquiring about what had happened. After some time he came back.

Tanya asked; 'What happened? Are you okay?'

'They've stopped the traffic for a while,' Ashu said. 'It seems someone has jumped off a cliff and died.'

'What! Who did such a stupid thing?'

'I don't know. I didn't ask. I felt uncomfortable standing there.'

'Are you okay? You look shaken.'

'I'm okay. But I don't think we should go there. I don't want to see these things.' He looked at her anxiously as if he was asking for her permission to leave.

'I think we should leave this place,' Tanya agreed. 'We can always come here again.'

'For sure.'

'Promise you'll bring me here soon?'

'I will. I promise,' Ashu said. And they turned around.

Chapter 20

He once again started driving, not knowing where he was going. He had made the same promise to Anshu a few months ago, but failed to deliver on it. Suddenly, a bike hit the rear of their car. Ashu stopped the car by a side of the road where a few people were gathered. He got out and immediately the two men sitting on the bike entered the car forcefully and asked him to get into the car as well.

'Get into the car or it's not going to be good for either of you,' one of the strange men said. Ashu did not think twice. He got into the car.

'Who are you and why are you doing this?' he asked.

The strange man did not say anything, but he dialed a number on his mobile and put the phone on speaker. It was Andy who picked up.

'Hey Ashu, my brother, how are you man? And how is my sweetheart dolly? I know you both were in that hotel last night. How was the night?'

They were both shocked. They could not fathom how Andy had got to them.

'What happened, Ashu?' Andy said. 'Did my sweetheart not satisfy you last night? Did both of you get enough sleep or were you playing all night with each other?'

'What do you want Andy?' Ashu asked.

'Both of you at my place. Otherwise...'

'Otherwise?'

'Otherwise my boys won't think twice to shoot you.' And immediately, one of the two strange men pressed a gun into Ashu's back in such a way that people outside could not see anything.

'Andy what the hell are you doing?' Tanya screamed. 'Are you mad?'

'Tanya, my sweetheart! So nice to hear your voice baby. But I wanna see you here soon, so I am going to hang up now. My boys will help you reach me. Don't do anything silly because some other people are following you too.' He laughed and disconnected.

They had no option but to be quiet now. Tanya started sweating even though it wasn't quite warm.

'What are you going to do with us?' Ashu asked.

'Drive you straight to Chandigarh,' one of the strange men said.

'Why not Delhi?'

'Because your friend is waiting in Chandigarh and we're going to take you there using a route that almost no one knows about.'

Ashu started driving. One of the strange men was guiding him through a road that was almost deserted. Ashu looked around.

'Tanya, where is your seat belt?' he asked.

One of the strange men said; 'No need of all that. You concentrate on driving.'

Ashu said again to her; 'I told you to wear your seat belt.' She stared at him angrily.

Ashu suddenly started driving faster. One of the strange men said; 'No need to go so fast!'

Ashu noticed in the rearview mirror that one of the strange men was searching for something on his phone. Ashu suddenly stamped on the brake pedal so that everyone in the car lurched forwards. The man sitting behind him with the gun also lost his balance completely. He fell in between Ashu and Tanya. Ashu did not waste a second. He held the man by his neck, took his gun, and set it against his head. Meanwhile, Tanya had recovered from the shock. She'd hit her head and was bleeding.

'Ashu, you idiot!' she said. 'What the hell were you…?'

He struck the strange man's head with the gun, knocking him unconscious. Meanwhile, the other man, the one sitting behind Tanya, had recovered too. He pulled out his gun and fired at Ashu. The bullet hit his left arm. He screamed and so did she. But he did not lose control. He jumped towards the man and hit him very hard on the face with the gun. The man fainted.

Ashu came out of the car, opened the rear door, and hit the man in the back seat on his head again. He threw both unconscious men out of the car.

He then noticed another car coming towards them. He knew it meant trouble. He got back into his car and started driving. The other car followed them. He drove fast. It was becoming a chase.

'Are they following us?' Tanya asked. He did not reply. 'Ashu, I asked you if they are following us.'

'Yes, I think so.' He drove on to the main road. The other car followed them.

She was worried. Then suddenly she noticed his left arm, which was bleeding. The bullet had taken out a very small piece of skin from his arm.

'Your arm is bleeding!' she cried. 'Stop the car!'

'Are you mad? They are following us!'

'They can't do anything now. We are on the main road. We have to find a hospital. Please stop the car.'

'Tanya,' Ashu snarled, now getting angry, 'shut your damn mouth. I'll slap your face if you say one more word.' She shut up after that. He stopped near a police booth.

'What are you doing?' she asked softly.

'I think we should call the police.'

'Andy will definitely have made a deal with them. I'm sure of it.'

He thought for a while about it and concluded that she had a point. They were very far removed now from their normal lives. *Blood, Shootouts, and fear of death...* They had seen it all. And it would have all been for nothing if Andy caught them now.

'Why are you thinking now, Ashu?'

Ashu held his wounded arm. 'Look Tanya, I don't know if I'm right or not, but now we have got into this so we have to play properly. If we will do, then we might get out of this alive, but if we give up now then we are surely going to die. Do you understand what I'm saying?'

He was looking like he was in real pain now. His eyes were getting red. He had lost a lot of blood. He was about to say something more, but she suddenly kissed his lips. The kiss lasted for almost ten seconds. She caressed his cheek.

'Shit. I'm sorry. I couldn't control myself.' She turned away. He smiled. 'I promise that I'm going to keep you safe,' Ashu told her. 'In my life, if I can be serious at any time, then this is going to be that time.' He kissed her again.

They had forgotten that they were standing near a police booth. Cops could catch them easily. They were badly injured too. But all this, still, didn't stop them. Ashu saw one cop coming in their direction. He immediately pulled himself away from her and drove away. The cops started following them on bikes, but they managed to escape them.

'You're really fast,' she said. 'How did you manage that?'

He smiled, but said nothing.

'By the way, what is the punishment for kissing at a public place?' Tanya asked. 'I mean, what is the fine?'

'I'm not worried about the kissing at a public place. I'm more worried about our wounds. They can take us to jail and then ask many questions.'

'I've never gone to jail,' Tanya said with a childish smile.

'You sound sweet to me. But you're actually talking bullshit.'

'I think we should get to a hospital,' she said. She saw one hospital and asked him to stop.

'No, we can't go there,' Ashu said. 'It's a famous hospital and if we go there they will ask for police verification because I've got bullet wound. We need a local doctor. They'll help us if we pay a little extra. And by the way, switch off your phone.' They both turned their phones off.

Ashu checked the car and found nothing suspicious. They found some local doctors and went to one of them. He quickly made a deal with the man for treatment without questions. Luckily, the bullet had touched his skin only. It was not inside his body. So he simply got some stitches and painkillers. They were about to leave that place when he suddenly noticed the wound on her forehead. It was a small one, but bad enough to hurt.

'What is this?' he asked. 'When did you get this? Shit, I didn't notice it.'

'Ashu, do you ever notice the pain of others? You always think only about yourself. I was sitting right in front of you, but you didn't notice my pain. And you say I'm your darling.' He felt bad, even though she said all this with a smile.

'I'm sorry, Tanya,' he said. 'It's not nearly enough I know, but I'm sorry. Let's go get you treated...'

While the doctor was treating her, he closed his eyes and thought.

She told me many times not to be indifferent and today I'm actually feeling bad for my indifferent behavior. I took responsibility for and I claimed that she's my darling, but I was so selfish that I got treatment for myself without even being aware of her wounds. Shame on me!

He shook his head. He was indirectly remembering Anshu again.

When he opened his eyes, Tanya was standing right in front of him. She was smiling. There was a white bandage on her forehead and on her right hand where she'd got some scratches.

'Did you miss me?' she asked childishly.

'I don't know whether to cry or laugh over your childish behavior, but yes I missed you a lot while you were getting treated.' He held her in his arms and kissed her head. They both got into the car. He helped her put on her seatbelt as her right hand was bandaged.

'Shall I say thanks?' asked Tanya.

'Just enjoy the music.' Ashu switched on the music and started driving.

'What to eat now? I think we're both hungry.'

'Why don't you stop thinking and start doing something for a change?' she teased. She had now started making fun of everything he was saying. That's something we never mind in the early phases of any relationship of course. Such behavior seems cute and romantic.

But she seemed reluctant to go outside so asked him to get something which they could eat in the car. He got them burgers and coffee.

She had difficulty holding things with her right hand. He told her not to worry. They shared one burger and he fed her. It was quite romantic. He took one bite and then gave her the next. They forgot all their fear and pain and started enjoying the moment.

'You were really brave in the car today,' Tanya said. 'How did you manage it? Did you ever get training on how to handle such situations?'

'Well, I'm born to fight,' Ashu said. They both laughed.

'Okay, jokes apart, I don't know how I managed it. Sometimes we do things we are not capable of doing in normal circumstances and that happens only when we have a strong desire to do something. That strong desire converts the impossible into the possible.'

'Where did you read that?'

'We can read all such things anywhere, but how many of us actually do it after reading? Hardly anyone. Today I understood one thing. It is very easy to feel brave sitting at home and reading these motivational lines and strength quotes, but when it comes to applying these in our actual lives, then we know true pain and fear. Today I felt that pain and fear. So from now on I'll never give any statement to anyone until I actually have experience of it myself.'

She looked at him curiously. 'You are changed. You are not the same Ashu I met some weeks ago.'

'I'm just trying to adjust to the situation. We always have two options in times of crisis. We can walk away and live life in our comfort zone. Or we can stay and try to adjust with the situation we are in. When we take the second option, it looks we've changed. I always took the first option. Even when I was kid, whenever I faced any situation that was challenging, I always went to hide behind my mom.'

'So what's changed now?'

'I don't know. Sometimes we change our paths after we are hurt in life – physically, mentally, or with regards to the heart. But change is inevitable and we have to change. It is good if we change by our own decision. Otherwise if fate would force us to change then we might require paying more than we have invested until the time.' She was smiling, but he was serious.

'But I'm confused,' he said. 'How did Andy find us?'

'It's strange,' Tanya agreed. 'Where do we go now?'

'We'll do what we did last night. Find a place to stay first. And then we'll decide what to do next.'

However, just as he started the car, he heard someone knocking on the glass of the window. A boy was standing outside. Ashu looked at Tanya and started driving off, afraid that it was one of Andy's men. But she stopped him.

'He's looking decent.'

The young boy outside was a local and he asked for lift. He was going to the market. They agreed to give him a ride.

'What's your name?' Ashu asked.

'Armaan,' the boy said.

'Aman?'

'Not Aman. Armaan.'

'Oh, sorry. So Armaan, you live here?'

'Yes I stay here on rent. I'm a student.'

'What are you studying?' Tanya asked with a smile.

'I'm a student of psychology,' Armaan said.

'That's great,' Ashu said. 'But can you please guide us to a hotel where we can spend the night?'

'Are you from Delhi?' Armaan asked.

'Yes. How did you know?' Ashu asked.

'I saw your car's number plate.'

'You have keen eyes.'

'Well, he's studying psychology after all,' Tanya said.

Armaan told them the way to an area where they could find two or three hotels after they dropped him off. They went to a hotel and asked for a room. This time they took only one room because they did not want to be separated in the face of all the problems they were facing.

The weather was cold. That area they were in was on the way to the beautiful valleys of Kullu and Manali. When Tanya came to know of this, she looked at him and smiled.

'Okay, we'll go there if everything is fine,' Ashu said.

'So we still have no plan.'

He started smiling and suddenly he started laughing. He gave her a tight hug. But one of the hotel people interrupted them suddenly.

'Please don't do this here,' he said. 'This is not your city. It's a small village.'

Ashu quickly apologized.

'Why are you laughing like a donkey?' Tanya asked.

'Have you ever seen a donkey laughing?' he teased 'Okay, you're asking the same question every time and I'm giving you the same answer. You are still running on hope. That's good and...'

They were standing on the road. There was silence everywhere. It was not like the cities where nightlife started after 9 pm. So they had no choice but to stay at the hotel and order some food, even though they were not hungry. This was the first time either of them were eating dinner so early.

'What is this lifestyle?' Tanya asked. 'It's so boring.'

'Well, it's the lifestyle here. Even in my hometown, this is how it is. This is their life and they enjoy it as we enjoy ours.'

They both finished dinner and took their medicines.

'So,' Tanya said, 'we are going to share one bed today. What plans with regards to that? She asked the question with a little smile on her face. He pulled her to him. Now they were very close to each other. She smiled at him and looked into his eyes.

They were getting closer to each other. Each could feel the breath of the other on their faces. Each of them started brushing their lips against the other's softly. Very soon, she lost her control. Now they were both kissing more passionately and aggressively. But he suddenly lost his passion and seemed reluctant about carrying on. He pulled his lips away from hers, but their lips were still touching. She was breathing very fast now since she was more passionate than him in this game of love – or lust. After few seconds she said; 'I love you.'

He kissed her nose, then her eyes, and ended up kissing her forehead. He gave her a tight hug, a very tight one, and said; 'I love you too.'

She put her head on his chest. They stayed like that for almost a whole minute, eyes closed. She opened her eyes. He did too. They looked at each other.

'I think we should sleep now. We have to get out of here tomorrow.' He said

'Are you sure?' Tanya asked.

He kissed her again. 'Yes.'

They switched on the TV and watched for a while. Then they went to sleep.

She seemed relaxed now, feeling secured, having full trust over him. They also started claiming that they love each other as they felt a pleasures feeling for each other. So they thought to be in love

She opened her eyes in the middle of the night, yawned, and looked around. But she did not find him next to her. She came out of the room, searched for him everywhere, and finally found him on the rooftop of the hotel. It was cold out there. He was standing in a corner, looking down. She went to him and spanked him from behind. He looked back.

'What are you doing here?' he asked. 'You should be sleeping.'

'Shut up,' she said. 'I should be asking you that.' She put her head on his shoulder.

'I'm not feeling sleepy, so I thought I'd come up here and get some fresh air,' Ashu said.

'Sweetheart, this is not the time for fresh air,' Tanya said.

'I'm just wondering if I made the right decision by leaving Delhi.'

'That was our decision, not yours,' she said. 'Whatever we've done, whatever we're doing and whatever we're going to do, it will all be our decision. Not yours, not mine.' She kissed his cheek. 'Shall we go down now?'

They both went back to the room and went to sleep again.

Chapter 21

They woke up at around 10 am, when the room service phone rang to announce breakfast. He ordered breakfast and asked her to get up and get ready. They ate and were ready to leave by 11:30 am.

But the question remained: where to go?

There was a call from the reception. Ashu asked her to wait for a moment. She agreed and started watching television. She kept changing channels and suddenly noticed that one of the local news channels was showing the photos of the two people who'd entered into their car yesterday. She was shocked to hear that they were both death. Ashu came back up and seemed nervous. They both started watching the news.

"Two local boys were killed brutally by a strange man who has taken a lot of money from them as well,' the newsreader was saying. 'The police found two guns at the scene of the crime and have sent the same to test for fingerprints. They believe this will help in the investigation. One of the locals who witnessed this event mentioned that the man who killed the two was driving a red car, but said he didn't notice the number because the killer drove away very fast. But he noticed that the car had a Delhi registration number. So the local police have started searching for the boy with this red car.'

He immediately switched off the television and closed his eyes. He covered his face with both hands. She called to him, but he did not reply.

Tanya said to him; 'Please open your eyes and look at me.' He did not reply still. She said; 'Please listen to me, you didn't do anything wrong. You were only trying to protect us.'

No,' Ashu said heavily, 'I never ever thought this would happen to me. I might have made mistakes, but I'm not a murderer.'

'Ashu first look at me! Please, for God's sake!' Tanya said.

He opened his eyes, looked up and then bowed his head again.

Tanya said; 'Look Ashu, whatever you did, you did to protect us from those bad people. And we are together, so why are you worrying? I know it's not easy to digest these things, but if you lose hope then we're dead. I need you, and I love you. Please look into my eyes.' He looked up. 'I love you,' Tanya said, 'and we are together. Please do not behave like this. If you collapse then what will happen to me? I cannot take even a single step without you now. You are my strength; please continue to be my strength.' She kissed his head and gave him a tight hug. He also held her tightly. 'I love you and this should give you strength,' Tanya said. 'Please don't fall like this.' He nodded, sniffed, and then went into the bathroom to freshen up.

Things were getting worst now. When he came out, he saw her standing by the window, thinking. He came to stand behind her, put his hands on her shoulders.

'The view is awesome, isn't it?' she asked.

'Yeah, it is.'

'These last few days, all our plans are failing. I thought we'd do something fun today, but...'

'We can still have fun,' Ashu said. She stared at him, but did not ask anything.

'Look,' he said, 'now we cannot go back because, if we do, we'll have to go through the place where we made this blunder mistakenly. So we have to go forward, into that valley. We have no other options left. We need to do one thing though, whatever money we have in the car we have to throw out because they think we've stolen it from those dead men. So even if we get checked by cops, we'll get through clean since they don't have the car number.'

Now their bond was growing stronger in the face of these adverse situations they were going up against.

'So shall we go ahead?' Tanya asked.

"We have no choice. Let's go.' They paid the bill and got into the car.

'We have to clean the car somewhere,' he said. 'There's blood everywhere.'

'What about the money?'

'Keep some in your bag. We'll keep some more in our pockets.'

'And the rest?'

'Throw it out.'

They decided to throw the cash out in some deserted place, not here. They started driving. Soon, he found a place to get the car cleaned and washed out at. It was a local area and people there hardly knew what was going on in the city.

He was good at making up stories and gave the boys cleaning up the car an idiotic excuse for the bloodstains in the car – one Tanya did not particularly like. Tanya herself meanwhile was breathing in some of the good, fresh air and enjoying the lovely weather. After the car was cleaned, he came to tell her they could go.

'What excuse did you give them about the car's condition?'

'It doesn't matter.'

'Tell me.'

Ashu laughed. 'Tanya, you really should spank my face before I tell you what I told to them.'

She stared at him. He went on; "I couldn't come up with any great excuse that they'd believe. They asked about the blood and why the seats were broken. And I told them. I told them that we had a sex in the car and since we were doing it for the first time, it messed up everything in the car.'

She was shocked. 'What!'

'Yes I couldn't think of anything else, so –'

She punched his stomach, hard. He cried out in pain. 'Tanya, I'm sorry. I know I did wrong. You can hit me again.'

'Ashu, you are a... I don't know what to say but did you really say that?'

'Yes.'

'You should be ashamed. What will they think of me now?'

'Who cares?'

She started walking away from him. He held her hand, but she forcefully pushed him away.

'I'm sorry sweetheart,' he said. 'Look at me, I'm injured. I need your support, and you are going away from me!'

'Go to hell,' she said. She went to sit in the car.

He went to the car, knocked on the window, opened the door, and asked; 'Can I come in?' She did not reply and turned her face in the other direction. He took the driver's seat and touched her arm, but she pulled away.

'Tanya, can I ask something?' he asked very slowly. She did not react. He asked the same question again, two or three times, but she was unmoved.

'You ordered me to go to hell,' Ashu said, 'but I really don't know the way. So please tell me how to get there so I can do what you want.'

She looked at him angrily for some time, but soon enough her expression started changing. She was struggling to hold back a smile. She turned her face away. He touched her arm again.

'Ashu, just drive and don't talk all this bullshit,' she said, pointing at him.

'Tanya,' Ashu said, 'if you wanna smile, then you can. I'll look away.'

She smiled, but she was still angry. 'You say another word; I'll break your head.'

They started driving again. As they climbed the hills, the weather changed completely. She closed the window. It was too cold now and she was shivering. They did not have any clothes for winter. They needed to buy some woolen clothes. He was about to say something, but a police siren cut him off.

They looked back. A police van was following them. They looked back and then looked at each other. They both saw fear in each other's eyes. Then they started looking in front. But they were afraid of the police van that had started coming very close to their car now. She put her right hand on his left, as it was shifting gears. Soon, the police van crossed them and went away. They both took a long breath. Her hand was trembling.

'Are you okay?' Ashu asked.

'Yeah. You?'

'Yeah.' They were both quiet for a few moments.

'Shall we have some tea?' he asked. She agreed.

They stopped at a local market and got some tea. He wanted to buy some woolen clothes; that was their main need at this time. She agreed. They went to a big shop and bought some woolen clothes for themselves. Tanya wore one of the sweaters immediately.

'You also wear yours,' she said. He declined to do so. She said; 'Don't be stubborn now. We can't afford to be unwell at this point of time, at least you can't. Do you get it?'

After that he put his sweater on.

They had lunch at a local roadside restaurant. He went to get tea and snacks for them, but when he came back he did not find her around that place. He looked around and noticed that she was standing some distance away and talking to someone on the mobile. He came to her and put his hand on her shoulder. She looked back with panic and immediately disconnected the phone.

'Tanya, what are you doing?' he asked. 'I told you not to use your mobile.'

'It's not mine. I borrowed it from the man sitting next to our table.'

'And he gave it to you just like that?'

'No I said I'd sleep with him in return.'

'What?!'

'Yes. If you can say bad things about me then why can't I?'

'Oh God. I did that to avoid trouble!'

'So you'll say anything about me?'

'Tanya, please understand the situation we are in and don't create problems for no reason.

'Wow Ashu. Great. Good line to finish with. Can't you be sorry?'

'Look, if we claim to love each other, then there should be no space for sorry and thanks. These are bullshit words, which have no relevance. If we actually commit a mistake, then we can't get away by saying sorry. And if somebody has actually done something for us, then "thanks" is a very inadequate word. Actually, those who do not want to correct their mistakes say sorry and get away. Similarly, those who do not have the guts to reciprocate someone's efforts say thanks and get away. These two words are a shield for those who run away from things in life. I know because I did it many times in my life. But right now, I am not running away from things. Did you get me?'

He spoke aggressively. She looked at him anxiously. He was about to say something more, but suddenly she came next to him and shut him up by putting her lips on his. They drew apart after a few seconds.

'Now I know how to shut you up,' Tanya said softly.

He calmed down, but they'd had a very bad argument. They went back to the restaurant to finish their tea. She returned the phone she'd borrowed.

'Okay, don't look at me like that,' she told Ashu. 'I didn't say anything wrong to him. I just told him that my battery was down and that I needed to talk to my family urgently.'

'You were talking to your family?'

'They were worried about me.'

'Do you miss them?'

'Yes.'

Ashu sighed. 'Did you like this place?'

'Yes, very much,' she said. 'I thought it was boring at first, but now I feel differently.' She smiled.

He wanted to ask her something but immediately stopped himself. She said; 'We still haven't thrown away the money we're carrying. I have a plan.'

He laughed. 'I'm glad. At least we have a plan now.'

'If we cannot take that money with us, then we can give it to the people who need it. Throwing money away for no reason would be a waste.'

'Yes, you're right. But how can we give it to someone unknown? And why would anyone take from us? It's risky and also money coming from bad sources will have bad effects. I've heard this many times from my elders. If we steal money, happiness or pleasure, and use it for our own benefit, it never gives us any benefit in the long run.'

'Tell me something,' Tanya said, 'you have tasted and tested everything in life. You drink, you smoke, and you have been to all the bad places. Does your family allow any of these things? I imagine not.'

'You are right,' he conceded, 'I never considered these things when I walked on incorrect path. But now I'm changing and everyone has the right to change.' He was quiet for some time and said; 'I agree with you. You know, that's a major problem with us. When we have to do something wrong and incorrect, then we don't think twice. But when it comes to do anything that is right then we have lot of dilemmas on whether to do it or not. Like what you are saying now may be right, but I have lot of questions on whether to do it or not.'

'Let's do it.'

'But not today. I don't want to go anywhere now. We'll stay here for tonight. What do you say?'

She agreed. They again arranged for a place to spend the night.

That night, after dinner, they spent some time on their balcony. It was cold, but since they were wearing woolen clothes, they did not mind it so much. She complained to him that the food had not been great.

'Would you really even care if the police caught us or if Andy killed us brutally?'

'Why are you talking about Andy now? Are you missing him? She teased.

'I'm serious. With everything that's going on now, you're talking about the food quality.'

'I don't understand you nowadays,' Tanya said. 'Suddenly you're serious and suddenly you're laughing. I don't know when to be serious and when to be laugh with you.'

'Now you are getting angry. I am just asking you to concentrate on important things. But your focus seems to be more on food and clothes.'

'Ashu, you really wanna fight now? Okay, let's close this argument. I think we should sleep now.' And with that, she went to bed. He sat on the balcony alone then, thinking about his behavior. In some corner of his heart, he felt she was right, that he was getting too impatient of late. But then again, she was not being serious about what was happening and was expecting him to take care of everything, wasn't willing to do anything herself.

But then he finally reasoned that she was just scared and relying on him to help her through what was going on. She had put her trust in him completely, on his ability to take care of her through any problem they faced...

He was now feeling the heat of a very famous conflict, which we all face and that takes us to the path of Change. Usually our personality consists of two things.

We normally call them Good and Bad, Angel and Devil, Right and Wrong. Different people call them in different way. However, at one time only one personality possesses us. We can be either good or bad and so on. It totally depends upon our will power that whom we adapt to.

Some people are possessed by that Devil, Bad or wrong part. They are normally those people who adopt the easy path in life and avoid the correct path. They try to get things easily in life and in this race; they normally do mistakes and finally collapse.

On the other side, those who are possessed differently are normally those who adopt the correct path in life. They finally get the success in their life if they keep patience. People who are possessed by Angel part but do not carry patience also collapse finally as their impatient behavior takes them to the door of Devil.

Both Angel and Devil fight inside us on daily basis but it depends whom we listen. Even if we are very much under control of Angel, Devil wakes up at least once in a day. Same happens if we are possessed by Devil, Angel wakes up once in a day.

So, good people always gets a trigger once on daily basis to be bad and similarly bad people always gets a trigger from good part to be nice once on daily basis. That is why Change is an inevitable part of our life and we always change, that's sure but which way that's always under consideration.

Therefore, an angel would always be an angel and a devil would always behave like a devil, it is not true. They change, we change as circumstances change. Nevertheless, change is tough but we should not forget one thing;

We have to dive inside the sea to get pearls in life. Standing onto the seashore with the expectation that tides will bring pearls for us would only waste our time and ultimately would give as nothing but frustration

He went to see her. She was sleeping – or pretending to be. He smiled and called her name, but she did not reply, did not even move. He called her name again, and now she opened her eyes. 'Can't you see I'm sleeping?'

'No. You're a terrible actor.' He pulled her to him.

'Ashu, you beast, behave yourself,' she cried. 'You're hurting me!'

'That's what I wanna do.' He took her in his arms and out onto the balcony.

'Isn't it beautiful?'

'You idiot. It's night. I can't see anything!'

'But half an hour ago you were enjoying this.'

'I was in a good mood then. That's gone now thanks to you. I want to go back to bed now.'

'Why is your good mood gone now, and what can we do to make it come back?' She said nothing. 'Okay, I have a plan now. Let's get married, have kids, and stay here forever.'

'Great plan. Can I go now?'

'Oh come on, why are you so angry? We're both under a lot of pressure here.'

'That's no excuse to hurt our loved ones. You can't throw stones at your family members at home when you are beaten or humiliated by someone outside the house.' She yelled

'Come on Tanya, you are taking this too far. Okay, can we leave it now? I will not say sorry, but I will try to work on it, I swear. You should be happy. I've finally I got a plan now.'

'And what's that?'

'Look, we are in the worst situation possible now. We have been accused of killing two people and stealing from them. The cops are searching for us and Andy will never stop searching for us. His network is very vast. He can get us at any time. So we can't go back. And we have nothing in front of us either.'

'So what's your point? Stay here?'

'Not stay here but fly from here. Tomorrow, we will drive to the nearest airport and take the very first flight out from there.'

'Where to?'

'It doesn't matter.'

'But…' She wanted to argue, but couldn't. They had no other choice given the situation really. So she agreed to his plan.

They did not know what was going to happen next, tomorrow. But at least they had a plan.

Chapter 22

They were both in a good mood the next day. As he started the car, she laughed.

'What happened?' Ashu asked.

'These past few days, we've been changing hotels like we change clothes.'

'Today I hope that routine ends,' he said. And they drove off.

They were driving along hilly roads that were difficult but exciting to navigate. She put her head on his shoulder and held his left arm so that she could relax. He played some soft music. He started overtaking cars, trucks and buses on the road. This disturbed her.

'Can you please drive properly? There's no one chasing us.'

'Actually there are a lot of people after me,' he joked.

'After us,' she corrected, spanking him playfully He kissed her hand

They were enjoying the drive. She opened the window to enjoy the weather. They continued driving for the next two hours without stopping and by now they were near an airport. They felt tired and hungry and so stopped to get some refreshments.

It was very cold outside. They were shivering. They wore all the woolen clothes they had. She wore a woolen cap that almost covered her face.

They stopped at a small roadside place. It was made up of a small kitchen and some tables and chairs. They took a table and ordered some noodles and tea. They were the only customer there for a while, until some boys on bikes came and took the seats next to them and ordered tea. They were also enjoying their time it seemed.'

The view here was beautiful. She wanted to go to the other side of the road so that she could look of the edge of the mountain. He went with her.

'It's so calm and peaceful here,' she said. 'I am feeling so good now. I do not know what situation we are in, but I'm feeling free and it is because of you. You've brought me here and it's perhaps the best place I've ever been to.' She looked into his eyes and smiled.

'You're looking like a doll in your woolen clothes,' Ashu smiled. 'Especially that woolen cap.'

'I know it looks cute. That's why I wore it. And you didn't tell me that it looks nice until now. Shame on you.'

'I'm a shameless person,' he laughed. 'How much money you've spent on us up until now! You have a big heart.'

'I have a very big heart you stupid boy. You can't measure it in terms of money, but if you must know, then it's around…' She started counting.

'Don't stress. You used your card to shop. Take out your phone and see the messages you got each time you paid a bill.'

'For that I'd need to call Andy because those messages go to him. He has a very big heart, at least when it comes to spending money on girls.'

They were both quiet for some time. But suddenly, something struck him. 'One second, one second,' he said. 'What did you say?'

'What?'

'You used a card given to you by Andy whenever we shopped?'

'Yes, but –'

'Why didn't you tell me this before?' he yelled. 'How could you be so stupid? Every time you used that card, the notification went to Andy! You insisted on paying every time, and I allowed you. How could I be so stupid? That's how he's been tracking us. He got the notifications each time you paid with your card. And he has links everywhere. He could easily have called a police station and told them his card had been stolen and was being used by someone else. He would have got all the details about your card from them then including the place you used it. Tanya, how could you be so stupid?"

'But how –'

'Oh shut up, Tanya,' he said loudly. 'This is your mistake and you are still trying to give me excuses.' He turned away. They were both quiet.

She looked at him, wanting to say something. But then she looked over his shoulder and her eyes filled with fear. She screamed; 'Ashu get down!'

It was too late. A big stone hit the back of his head and he fell down. He was still conscious though. The strange boys who had been sitting next to their table were actually Andy's men.

They had been following them ever since they'd left the hotel that morning. Once again, her foolishness had put them in trouble. Ashu was right about how Andy had found them. He used his legal contacts and reached out to the shop in Chandigarh. Moreover, Tanya had stupidly told the shopkeeper the name of the hotel they were staying in that night. It became easy for Andy to track them from there. But his plans had been foiled when Ashu had shown his heroism in that incident in the car.

Both the strange men he'd sent after them had been half-killed by Ashu and Andy had done the rest. He killed the two men and also complained to the police. Now, thanks to Tanya's foolish behavior, Ashu was lying on the roadside with new strange men standing over him. Tanya looked shocked.

The guy who had hit Ashu was about to hit him one more time, but she pushed him away forcefully before he could. She wanted to hold Ashu, but she slipped and fell off the edge of the mountain. She only fell a few feet though.

Ashu tried to stand up. He had to be braver now than he'd ever been in his life. She was on her knees and was trying to get back up. He held out a hand to help her up.

As she reached out to take it, she screamed again; 'Ashu, look back!'

The two guys were coming towards him. They took hold of him and took him to where she was. This point was a few meters away from the road so no one could see. A third guy came over to join them.

One of the three guys warned them; 'It will be fine if you both cooperate.'

'Are you planning to throw us from here?' Ashu asked. They ignored him. Soon, one of the guys went back on to the road and saw someone coming that way. It was Andy.

Andy was looking happy to have finally caught them. He came down and thanked the guys who'd found them. Both Tanya and Ashu stood up when he came. He did not look at Ashu and went to her first. As he drew near her, his expression started to change. He was beginning to look angry.

He came close to her and slapped her very hard. It was a really bad blow. She fell down and lost consciousness for a few seconds. Ashu immediately reacted, tried to catch him but the two men held him tight. She was regaining consciousness. She tried to stand up but fell down again. She started crying. Ashu yelled; 'Andy, leave her alone!'

Andy smiled. 'Ashu! My brother and best friend! Why are you worrying about her? She's a hound. Don't worry. She'll manage.'

'I swear, I'll break your face.'

'I know man. I have no doubts you'll kill me as you promised. That's why I have no intention of letting you go.'

'At least help her up. Please. It's a request.'

Andy held out his hand to her, but she refused to take it.

'No man,' Andy said to Ashu. 'She's not interested in taking my hand. But she is using everything I gave her, strangely. Anyway, no problem. Tell me what you wanna do now. You want to get away from this place. But how? By car?"

He took Ashu to the road. Ashu's car was not there. One of Andy's guys had taken the key from his pocket and taken the car away.

'Now both of you can come with me I think,' Andy said. 'You have no option. So can you go down now and get that hound girl?'

He thought for a while and then went down. He pulled her into his arms. She looked at him and started crying. He kissed her head and held her close. She was still weeping. He helped her get up. She'd hurt her leg when she slipped, but she managed to stand. They both sat in Andy's car without any argument. They had no choice now but to do what he told them to. The driver started the car.

Chapter 23

Andy's driver was taking them back the way they came. She was looking outside, thinking about how much things had changed for them in such a short while.

Things were worse than ever for them and neither of them knew what Andy was going to do. He was looking calm. Both Tanya and Ashu were injured badly, but their wounds were not hurting them too badly as a wound sometimes behaves like a bad relation, it gives pain only when we give preference to it.

Ashu asked; 'Where are we going and what you are going to do to us?'

Andy looked at him, but didn't reply.

'Look Andy, we can't do anything now –'

'That's what I thought, until you killed two of my guys.' Andy snarled

'I didn't kill anyone. You know that. I can't do it. But I'm sure you can fix this…'

He talked to him without any fear, but she knew he was afraid. Andy looked at him for some time and then asked the driver to take a different route. Now they were going to some unknown place. Soon they reached at a piece of land with a very old house on it. Two local guys came from inside and they tried to take them both.

'Leave her,' Ashu yelled. He looked at Andy and said; 'Look Andy, we won't do anything stupid. She can't even walk properly. Believe me.'

Andy looked at him with a strange smile on his face and allowed him to hold her. They were taken to a room. Ashu helped her sit down. Andy watched all of this.

Then he said; 'Ashu, come outside with me. We need to talk. And I'm not asking you, I'm telling you. Don't worry about her. She's not going anywhere without my permission, and she won't go anywhere without you because she needs you now.' Andy stared at her, but she ignored him completely and turned away.

'Okay,' Ashu said.

'Ashu, don't go with him,' Tanya said. 'He's not your friend and can do anything.'

Ashu told her not to worry and they both went outside.

'Tell me,' Ashu said.

'Is this really you man?' Andy asked. 'The one who used to be so carefree? What are you doing, throwing your life away for a girl like her? I used her many times and I don't know how many boys she slept with before meeting me.'

'Look Andy, I'm in your custody but that doesn't mean I'll listen anything. Let this be the last time you insult her in front of me. Next time you do, I'll kill you. I don't care.'

Andy laughed; 'You've already done enough damage to your life. I will give your car to the police and they will go to your house in Delhi and then to your hometown itself. Your family will know what you did. Then imagine what would happen.'

'Are you threating me?'

'No I'm telling you, what I can do. I am giving you a choice. You can walk out of this now. I have no bad feelings towards you. I only need her because she betrayed me. I'm not like those fools who accept apologies for such a mistake. You can meet me at Delhi and we can again enjoy ourselves together like brothers. But if you choose to remain involved then…'

'I choose to remain involved,' Ashu said defiantly.

Andy raised a hand, but then stopped. He looked at Ashu thoughtfully. 'What would you have done if you escaped? Marry her?'

'I'd never let her go.'

Andy pulled Ashu by his arm, back into the room. He then went out and locked the room from outside. Ashu shook his head.

She was searching for something on her mobile when he came in. She tried to hide it, but Ashu said; 'Don't worry. You can use it now.'

'What did he say?' Tanya asked anxiously.

'Nothing. Just bullshitting.' She kept looking at him. 'I mean it sweetheart. He really said nothing.'

'After a long time you're calling me sweetheart,' Tanya smiled. Some blood was oozing out of her forehead. He wiped it off.

'I called you that just last night.'

'I know. But when we are happy, years pass like days. And when we're sad, even days feel like months.'

'Whatever. As long as you're smiling,' he said.

They both became quiet now. He closed his eyes, but it seemed as if he was thinking about something very serious.

'I know we are in trouble because of me,' she said sadly.

He opened his eyes. 'No doubt about that, but we can fight about it later. This is not the time to fight or blame each other. This is the time to be together and think together.'

'Do you think we can get out of here?'

'I don't know. But don't worry. We'll figure something out.'

Her eyes started getting wet now. 'Do you really love me?'

'No, I'm mad and I always carry away every girl I meet with me and face fatal situations,' he replied sarcastically.

'But why? I've only caused you trouble since the beginning. And I've never done anything to make you happy.'

'I think I've now understood how to get pleasure from love. I never felt this way before about anyone though I spent a lot of time with many girls and one of them actually changed my life before leaving me. Actually, I threw her out of my life...' He took a long breath

'Who?'

'Anshu.'

'Oh so Anshu is your ex-girlfriend.'

'Yeah. But she doesn't deserve to be the ex of any boy. I don't know why God doesn't think about people like Anshu. Why he lets girls like Anshu meet with boys like me. She was unlucky to have me in her life but I was lucky to get a chance to spend some time with a girl like her. She deserves the best in the world... And I know she'll get that one day.'

'Did she ever put you in a situation like this?'

Ashu laughed. 'In fact, I always put her in stupid situations. She used to get angry when I made mistakes, but she always saved me. She was physically small, but she would always shield me from anything and anyone. Though I was financially better off than she was, she never let me spend any money because she wanted me to stop wasting money. She was... great.'

His expression was different when he talked about Anshu. He was excited, laughing, but still feeling a pain inside.

'So you behaved with her the way I'm behaving with you now,' Tanya said. 'And you're doing for me what she did for you.'

He started laughing loudly, but he did not say anything. He caressed her face. 'I can't ever be her. I'm just trying to be.'

'Do you still love her?' Tanya asked.

'No, I don't. In fact I've never loved any girl before. I used to be a real bastard and that's why people like Andy always liked me, because they belonged to the same category. Now I'm feeling for you the same thing she used to feel for me. Now I know the irritation and pain I caused her. But I promise that I'll never let you down in life. It might not be the first time I am making this promise to a girl, but this time I really mean it and I'll make good on it.'

'You can get better than me, Ashu,' Tanya said quietly. 'I'm giving you only pain and nothing else.'

'You can get better too. But that doesn't mean we leave what we have. Searching for better options sometimes takes us on secluded path'

She was about to say something, but the door opened then. It was one of Andy's guys. He came inside the room, checked something and then left. But he did not lock the door.

'We need to get out of here,' Ashu said.

'How?' Tanya asked. 'We don't even know where we are and it could be dangerous.'

'Andy is wasting his time. He should have killed us both. I would have done it in his place. But he hasn't done anything so far. I know him. He is an elusive man. He might have some other plan.'

Ashu opened the door. There was a dead silence about that place. He went out onto the road. There was no one there. Ashu turned around and started running very fast, back towards the house. He was surprised to see his car parked behind the room. He was very confused now.

He went back to the room she was in. 'What's happening?'

'Did you hear anyone parking the car?'

'No. What happened?'

'I don't know, but we have to get out of this place immediately. There's no one outside. Wait, let me check again. You stay here.'

He went outside to inspect his car. There was some money spread out on the back seat. He was surprised to see a gun placed on the driver's seat. He took the gun excitedly, but then threw it away. He had made a mistake, he realized.

You fool! You touched it and now it has your fingerprints all over it. You should have understood his game. He is not doing anything to you directly. He is trapping you very smartly. And you touched the gun. You are as big an idiot as she is.

He controlled himself, took her bag, and put some money in it. He also took all the documents from the car which could disclose his identity. He went back to the room.

'We need to go, Tanya. Take your bag.'

'What happened?'

'Don't ask questions. I don't have answers.'

He was about to say something, but before he could they heard the noise of some vehicles. He pulled Tanya by the hand and they both went out of the room. But they were shocked to see two police jeeps coming to a stop right in front of the gate. They looked at each other and realized they could not go through the front gate. He took her out back.

'Are we not taking the car?'

'No, we can't.'

He noticed that the back wall was not so high. It was about five feet tall. He asked Tanya to jump over the wall but she couldn't because her leg was hurt.

He took her bag and threw it on the other side. Then he took her in his arms and set her on top of the wall. Then he himself jumped over the wall and landed on the other side of it, onto a road.

She hurt herself while jumping. He gave her a tight hug. Her heart was pumping very fast now.

They walked down the street which took them to a local market. It looked like a village but still, it was an unknown place.

They started walking, but she was not feeling well due to her injuries. She was not able to walk properly, but they had no choice but to move on.

He observed two cops jumping onto the street from behind the same wall, as they had. It seemed they were searching for them. He held her hand and wanted her to speed up, but her body was not allowing it.

'We have to move fast. They are searching for us.'

She looked back nervously. The cops were searching. Ashu and Tanya tried to blend into the crowd.

'Are they still coming?' Tanya asked.

'I can't keep looking back. They'll get suspicious. We need to get away from here. Our outfits are different from those of the locals. They're definitely going to be on to us soon.'

'You're sure they're searching for us?'

'Very sure.' He looked back and then pulled her in a different direction, into a very congested street that did not even have any proper lighting. They kept walking and emerged into a wide area.

It looked like a farm, with a wall running around it that was about four feet high. He looked at her.

'No,' she said. 'I can't jump now. Please, I really can't.'

He again picked her up and put her on top of the wall. He crossed that wall easily and then brought her down from the wall. They sat behind the wall and hid themselves so that nobody could see them. She was tired. He took her in his arms and asked her to relax for some time. She put her head on his shoulder.

It looked like she was relaxing. But her heart was beating very fast. She started easing up, but he was still tense. They were in that position for almost fifteen minutes.

He suddenly opened his eyes and looked at her. He called her, but she did not reply. He put his lips very close to her ears and then called her again.

'Are you sleeping?'

She opened her eyes. They were full of fear. 'Don't worry,' Ashu said. 'We'll get out of this. Trust me.'

'I know. I trust you.'

'We cannot stay here for long. The cops will try their best to catch us. After all, we have been accused of killing two people. We'll be more than lucky if we get out of this place and situation alive and free. This is the reality.'

'At least say something positive about the situation, even if it's a lie,' Tanya said laughing.

They got up and started walking away from that place. They came to the street. He asked her to wait there while he found the way to the highway. He came back after ten minutes.

'Well?'

'I found the way, but we'll have to walk I'm afraid. We have no choice.'

'Can't we stay here tonight?

'No. This is a village so we won't find any hotel here. Once we reach the highway we can find a place. So let's go.'

They started walking. 'What if the cops are there?'

'They won't be. They won't imagine we took this route.'

Soon they reached a flat road. They saw a bus stop and people standing there. Ashu was relieved. A bus arrived soon. They got into it.

'How long?' she asked.

'Half an hour. I asked the conductor and he said the bus will drop us at a place where we can find somewhere to stay.'

There were a few people sitting in the bus with them. She held his arm and rested her head on his shoulder. 'I'm going to sleep. Let me know when we get there.' He caressed her cheeks.

He closed his eyes too.

And then suddenly some cops got into the bus from the front door. He asked her to get up so that they could run away. But the cops were too fast. They caught and held them both and asked the bus driver to drive to the police station.

The cops asked them to cooperate. One of the cops was staring at her and smiling.

Ashu didn't like that. 'Why are you laughing?' he asked.

The cop replied; 'Tell me one thing. What did you get in return for helping this girl? You are going to die soon.' All the cops laughed.

That was too much noisy for him; specifically their last words "You will die soon" were making trouble for his ears frequently. He looked at her and saw that she was smiling. He was shocked. Suddenly the bus stopped and a ray of light touched his face.

He opened his eyes.

He'd been dreaming.

He looked around. Nobody was there. He looked at her. She was sleeping on his shoulder. He was sweating and breathing very fast but soon he calmed down. He called to her. She opened her eyes. 'Wake up,' he said. 'We are almost there.'

They saw some hotels soon. The driver stopped the bus and Ashu thanked the conductor who'd shown them this place.

They got a room to stay in. They were now feeling very tired. Their bodies were hurting all over. They took their medicines, some painkillers especially so that they could relax. They ordered some food and she asked him over dinner; 'What are you thinking about? Aren't you hungry?'

'Thinking about today. Nothing else.'

'Okay, you keep thinking. But I'm not in a position to think about anything now,' she smiled.

He was glad to see her smiling. That's all he wanted, to make her happy. But the situation was not allowing him to make her happy all though was trying his best to handle it. After dinner, they sprawled on the bed. She soon fell asleep, but he was not able to. He stood up, went to the window, and gazed outside.

His expressions were changing by the minute. He was sad, then smiling, and then sad again. He started shaking his head.

'It's not easy to behave like you did,' he said softly. 'And it's not easy to endure someone like me. I've understood this now. So thumbs up to you, Anshu. You endured me until the very end you wanted to be with me for even longer, but I was such a... such a...'

He could not finish as his emotions were getting the better of him now. He took a long breath to control his emotions and bowed his head for few seconds.

'I'm sorry Anshu,' he said again. 'I'm really sorry... Look at me. I'm saying sorry now and thinking that a simple word can erase the mistakes that I made with you. But I need you now to save her. Please guide me...' His voice was thick with sadness. His eyes were full of tears.

He closed his eyes then and started smiling.
"Hum Jo Thae Woh Reh Na Sake
Kuch Bhi Kisi Se Keh Na Sake
Badalne Ki Khwaahish Thi Iss Dil Me
Isliye Tumse Judaa Reh Na Sake
Tere Kadmo Ke Nishaan Dhundhate Hain Hum
Fir Mohabbat Ki Khwahish Me Doobate Hai Hum
Ab Doobana Hai Yaa Paa Lena Hai Saahil

Mar Jaana Hai Ya Karna Hai Khud Ko Haasil"
(I started changing differently but
Couldn't say anything to anybody
Since my heart wished for changing track
So couldn't get apart from you
I keep searching for your footsteps so that
I could easily swim in the sea of love
Now whether I will sink else will get the shoreline
Whether I'll die else will find myself "

Today, they had escaped from both Andy and the police. The escape from Andy's clutches had probably been by chance. But the way they'd gotten away from cops, that was brave indeed - especially since they'd both been physically beaten. Now their problem was how to move ahead. They'd lost their car. So how were they going to get around? They had to think about it. However, for now, they were safe.

Was their luck finally turning or was this just a lull before the storm? Only time would tell. He fell back into the bed and tried once more to fall asleep – but in vain.

'No dreams come to a sleeping mind when we see dreams in our waking hours and still ignore them.'

Chapter 24

They did not dream that night. And when they woke up the morning, their bodies were still hurting even though they had taken painkillers. She was standing in the balcony. He put his arms around her from behind, but she did not react.

'What happened?' he asked. 'You look nervous. It's morning.'

'Nothing,' she said, 'I've ordered breakfast. So get ready.'

He turned on the TV so that they could watch something.

They were surprised to see one of the local new channels carrying the news about the two men who had been killed some days ago near Chandigarh. The news was not in their favor.

'The Police found the red car from Delhi. The local police believe that the car belongs to the same man who killed the two men some days ago. They also found some money in the car, which the killer had taken forcefully from the two victims. The police found the car at a farm but unfortunately the killer escaped before the police arrived. But the police are searching for him and will surely get him very soon.'

He started smiling, but she seemed nervous.

'What happened?' he asked. 'Why are you nervous?'

She pointed at the television.

'No point worry about it,' he said. 'We have to face it. We got ourselves into this mess. The first thing we need to do is leave this state as soon as possible.'

'That's what we've been trying to do!' she cried. 'Every day a new problem comes up –'

'There's only one other thing we can do. We can go to the police and tell them the truth.'

'No way!' she said.

'Well then we have only one other option left. And that is to get out of this state quickly. We need to reach my hometown so that we can come up with some final solution. Only my family can help us now. Only they can understand our problem. Look, we did not do anything wrong. We left Delhi because Andy was torturing you mentally and physically. We can prove it. If we killed those two men, then that was in self-defense. The money that was found in our car belongs to Andy and that we can prove together.' He held her hand. 'I don't know what is right and what is wrong anymore. But at this point of time, we both need each other. We'll get out of this situation if we're going to be sailing together. I don't know about you, but I need you very badly now.

So be with me mentally and physically.'

Andy was smart enough to leave them be right now because he knew they'd try to run away from the police and that would ultimately make them look guilty in the eyes of the law.

Why kill the one who is ready to commit suicide? Andy figured.

Tanya and Ashu left the hotel. 'So we have a place to go to now,' Tanya said, 'but it's strange.'

'What is strange?' he asked. 'You should be happy.'

'Yeah. But when we didn't have any place to go, we were enjoying. Now when we finally have a destination, I'm feeling anxious. Isn't it strange?'

'I didn't get your logic, but I'll assume that whatever you are saying is correct. And I feel that something is going to happen today.'

She looked him up and down, but said nothing.

They started moving. Their biggest problem was how to reach the airport. They decided to get a bus or taxi.

But as they reached the road, they saw a police van coming very fast towards them. They turned back. They both saw fear in each other's eyes. But the police jeep was not looking for them and it moved on ahead.

'We can't go together. We have to stay apart from each other,' Ashu said.

'What? What are you saying? Half an hour ago you were asking me to stay with you physically and mentally and now you're saying we need to stay apart?'

'Yes. That's exactly what I'm saying.'

'Are you sure?'

'Yeah. But we have to think this through.'

He held her hand, crossed the road, and asked her to sit on a big stone. He put both his hands in his pockets and started thinking. He looked at her. She was playing with her mobile. He again started thinking. They stayed that way for almost fifteen minutes. He went up to her.

'Look Tanya,' he said, 'I'm not leaving you, but I think moving together may be risky because I've not heard anything so far about that the person who killed those two men having any girl with him. So I think they are unaware that we are together. So, for safety purposes, we need to do it. I'll be around you, but not like this...'

'But –'

'It's only for a while. And I promise that I'll die before leaving you alone for even a single second. But please, we have to do it, for your safety... For our safety... You got it?'

He held her face in his hands. She took a long breath and nodded her consent.

'So how do we go now?' she asked. 'Bus? That'll be easier to get. And it's safe.'

'Yeah. That should be fine. And let's switch on our mobile phones.'

They waited at a bus stand but were standing away from each other. After some time one bus arrived at the stand. She got into the bus, but as he made to get into it, he saw some cops sitting in the bus. He suddenly abandoned the idea of taking this bus. The bus started to move ahead. She looked back anxiously, but the driver kept driving onwards.

She called him. 'What happened?' she asked.

'There were some cops sitting in that bus. But don't worry, I will take the next bus. You get there and wait. My phone battery is low so I'm switching it off. I will call you in a while.'

'Okay.'

He waited at the bus stand, wondering if he'd done the right thing by send her off alone. *Oh shit man. I did the wrong thing. I should've taken that bus. She's alone now and she's injured. She's my baby and I've left her alone just to save myself.*

He hit his own head and looked very annoyed. The other local people standing at the bus stand with him were staring at him. Some of them were laughing.

He switched his phone on and started dialing her number. He suddenly got a call from his roommate, which he disconnected. He dialed her number again. It was ringing, but then suddenly his battery died.

Noooooo… Not now… Oh God, this is not fair!

He was so angry and annoyed that he threw his phone away and screamed; 'No man!'

People around him started staring at him, but nobody interrupted him – perhaps because they were enjoying all his drama. He suddenly realized that he had made a very big mistake by throwing his phone away. It was the only connection between him and Tanya in this strange place. He went to retrieve his phone. Only some broken parts remained. He knelt down and started searching madly in the dust. He was looking for his sim. He managed to find it finally, along with his memory card. He collected all the parts of his phone.

He started laughing, looking up at the skies. Then he looked down and put a hand on his forehead. His hand then slid down and covered his face from chin to nose. He was not crying, but his eyes were wet. He closed his eyes and a few teardrops poured through them. But he was still smiling and shaking his head. It was sheer frustration

He had lost his patience at this critical point and now he was paying for it. He could not call Tanya. But when he turned back, he noticed that everyone around was looking at him. He started shaking his head and smiling. But an old man came up to him and asked; 'What happened child? Is everything all right?'

He initially felt irritated, but managed to control himself. He did not reply though. Then he felt the old man caress his head as if he was blessing him. Ashu stared at him. The old man offered him water, but he declined. He thought for a while, and then stood up and smiled at the old man. He looked away. And then suddenly he saw Anshu in the crowd. He blinked and looked again, but she was gone then. It was all unknown faces once more. His heart started pumping very fast now.

He had to contact her. An idea came to him. He could borrow a phone from someone around him. He asked a few people but they all denied him. They were all looking a little afraid of him. His clothes were dirty because of the dust. In fact even his face and hands were dusty. Then he noticed the old man who'd offered him water going away from that place. Ashu ran to him.

'Uncle, can I use your phone to make one call please? Mine is lost. Please, it's urgent.'

The old man thought for a few seconds and then replied; 'I have balance for only a few calls which I need to make to my family in case anything happens to me. I'm very old and I've come out of my house to walk for some time.'

Ashu became sad and turned to leave. The old man thought for a while again and then stopped him. 'Wait ... Hang on... It seems from your condition that your urgency is more than my own. So you can call.'

Ashu was overjoyed. He took the phone, dialed her number. It started ringing. But she cut the call. He dialed again, but with the same result. He waited for one minute and then dialed again, but now her phone was switched off. He dialed again after few seconds, but with the same result. After many failed attempts, he returned the phone to the old man and said; 'Thanks for your help. At this age, I am supposed to be the one helping you, but I took your help. Thanks again, I'll never forget this.'

The old man put his hand on his shoulder and said; 'Look child, help is something that should be given to all those who need it. A precious gift sometimes wipes away our sins if we give it to the person who actually needs it. We should never waste it by throwing it to someone who doesn't need it. Therefore, if you find two needy people, then you need to look at them and judge their urgency irrespective of gender, age, and physical competency. Never waste help.' The old man smiled; 'May God always keep you happy.'

Ashu looked at the old man walking away until he could see him no more and swore that he would never forget what he'd told him.

He then turned back and started looking for a shop to buy a new mobile from. He walked around for twenty or twenty-five minutes and found a suitable place. He bought a basic mobile phone that was not very costly. He switched on the phone and tried her number again, but with no success. He was not able to understand why her phone was not reachable though he'd clearly told her to keep her phone on all the time so that they could be in contact with each other.

He kept trying her phone for the next half hour. But it kept saying switched off. He decided to follow her.

A bus arrived and he took a seat inside it. Only one question was bothering him: *Why did she switch off her phone?*

The bus started heading out. Ashu was looking very depressed now. He placed his head on the glass of the window and started looking outside.

The bus he was travelling in soon stopped because there was some disturbance on the road. Another bus had got into an accident on the road. He became anxious, got out of the bus very fast, and went to the place of the accident. He asked an eyewitness about the accident.

'There were few people sitting in the bus,' the man said. 'The driver tried to avoid a car that was coming from the other side of the road. That's what caused the accident. But all the passengers are okay except one lady who was injured.'

Ashu looked around, but did not see her. He asked about the woman who was injured. The same eyewitness told him that she was getting treated at a clinic nearby. He did not think twice and ran to the clinic. It took him around fifteen minutes to get there. He took a deep breath when he saw the injured woman. She was not Tanya. He started heading out of the clinic, but the doctor asked; 'Are you with her?'

'No, I don't know her,' Ashu replied.

'She seems alone and new to this place. She is badly injured.'

Ashu did not react and started getting out of the clinic, but he suddenly stopped and turned back.

'Could you please allow me to meet the lady who's injured?' Ashu asked the doctor.

'But you said you didn't know her?' the Doctor asked.

'I just want to see how she is and see if there's anything I can do to help her as she is all alone.'

'I appreciate that,' the Doctor said admiringly.

He met with the woman and learnt that she belonged to a different village but had come here to meet someone. She'd lost her mobile in the accident so she could not call her family as she did not remember any of their numbers. But she was sure the phone would be somewhere near the site of the accident.

He did not think twice and went to the place of the accident. He searched the bus, but did not find anything. He then asked for the place where they'd found the injured woman. He reached that point and found what he wanted. Nobody had picked it because it had fallen between two stones. He'd found it only because he'd been searching for it.

He went back to the clinic. The injured woman was happy to see her mobile. She called her family. She was crying while talking to her husband and explained what had happened to her. Ashu felt better now. He smiled and made to leave.

'Thank you brother,' the woman called after him.

'I did not do anything,' Ashu smiled. 'It was all fate. By the way, who is coming to take care of you?'

'My husband.'

'Okay,' he said and walked away.

He went out and took a deep breath. He was smiling. He had never ever helped anyone like that. He'd come out of his comfort zone for the first time in his life to help someone. But suddenly he felt nervous. He thought about Tanya. He looked up at the skies.

Oh God, if she's in the same position, then please send someone to take care of her because I'm not there. If I did something right now then I don't want this to be counted in my list of good deeds. Please help her in return for this. I know I am being selfish. But please do it for me and help her...

He realized then that he had to get a bus. He controlled his emotions and reached the nearest bus stand. He was lucky enough to get another bus very soon and took a seat. He tried her number again, but in vain.

Suddenly, another thought occurred to him. He dialed another number. The person he was calling picked up very fast, on the first ring in fact. It was Andy.

'Hey man,' he said. 'Are you still –?'

'Where is she?'

'Who?'

'You know who. Don't act stupid with me.'

'Are you asking about Tanya? If so, then I should be the one asking you that. You're the one who took her away from me.'

'She was never a part of your life. I don't want to listen to any more of your bullshit and I'm asking you seriously. Where is she?'

'She left you too? Are you serious?'

'Okay, she has left us both now. So let's meet now. Either you come to me, or you tell me where you are and I'll come to you. What do you say?'

'I can destroy your life now you know,' Andy yelled.

'You've already done enough damage to my life. Now please come and do whatever you wanna do with me. You always say that you can do lot of things. Now I'm asking you to hurt me as badly as you can. If you have the guts, then you will not deny me.'

'What happened to you? You're sounding abnormal.'

People around were continuously staring because he was screaming now. Ashu stared back at them, but then he controlled his anger and asked the driver to stop the bus and got out immediately. Again, he asked Andy to meet him. Andy agreed this time and asked for his location. They agreed to meet in two hours. Ashu tried her number again. It was still switched off.

He was confused now. Not knowing what had happened to her was the worst kind of torture. He was supposed to display some mature behavior at this time, but he lost his way and was now waiting for Andy instead of looking for Tanya.

At 5 pm, he noticed Andy's car reaching the place. He was standing by the side of the road, a little away from the road in fact.

Andy got out of his car. Ashu was not looking at him. He knew that Andy had arrived, but did not turn back. He sensed Andy coming towards him and he finally turned around to look at him. He started moving now towards Andy with a little smile on his face.

They neared each other. Ashu's expression changed completely. He screamed and hit Andy on the face. It was a very hard blow and was enough to knock him unconscious. Suddenly, two people got out of the car and held Ashu. They took him to the side of the road. One of them held him from behind and the other one started landing punches on his face and stomach. His attempts at escaping were useless. They were more powerful than he. They were continuously beating him and he was not reacting. It seemed he had given up. Soon, Andy recovered consciousness. He stood, wiped the blood from his face, and came to them.

He was angry, but when he saw his boys beating Ashu, his anger lessened. Andy ordered his people not to beat him and asked them to step away. He took a gun from one of them and put it against Ashu's head. Then he saw Ashu's pathetic condition and pulled him up by the neck.

'What are you doing this for man?' Andy asked. 'For a girl who is nothing but a...'

'Andy, I'll break your face if you say anything about her,' Ashu said.

'Ashu, you are a fool,' Andy said. 'Look at you and your condition. You are gone brother. I wanted to kill you, but you've killed yourself my friend –'

'Oh shut up!' Ashu yelled. 'We're not friends. We're not brothers. You've destroyed me. You have made me a killer and now the police are behind me because of you. You told them and planned to trap me for all the crimes I never committed.'

'I didn't do anything wrong to you,' Andy yelled back. 'When you first ran away with her, I asked you to leave her. But you didn't. You killed two of my men just for her, intentionally or unintentionally. Even at the farmhouse I asked you to stay away from that damn girl, but you didn't. Your decisions have destroyed your life. I was trying to catch her because she betrayed me. You came in between us every time. You are a fool man. A bloody fool!'

'I love her,' Ashu said. 'And I'll come in between you two every time. You know what your problem is? You always meet and stay with bad people. That is why you think like this. I was also like you once, but in the last one year, I had the chance to meet some beautiful people. Those people were decent as they were caring and dedicated towards their loved ones and even towards those who were unknown to them. You won't understand this as the phase you are in is like a furore that gives us nothing but an exaggerated zeal. We like it because it gives immense pleasure. It takes us to the top not because we deserve to be there but just to push us down from the highest point so that, when we fall, then it's all over… I've already gone through this phase in my life. It gives immense pleasure for some time but it is life-sucking.' He was looking deep into Andy's eyes.

'Okay,' Andy said, 'I agree that I'm bad and that I live with bad people. But one thing I never forget is friendship and brotherhood. We all always live like brothers. I always treated you like my younger brother. I also loved her a lot, in my own way. That was my style of expressing love and I don't regret it. She betrayed me and I might catch her one day. But right now I came for you. Leave everything and come with me.'

He stood up and held out a hand. 'It's an offer from a brother to a brother,' he said.

They both were looking into each other eyes. Andy soon realized that he would not accept his hand. He thought for a while, smiled, and then asked; 'Why did you hit me?'

'Because you hit her that day,' Ashu said. Andy started laughing very loudly looking at skies.

'You are too much,' Andy said. 'I can't kill you. Nobody can kill you. You are already dead man.'

He held Ashu's face in his hands and looked into his eyes but he saw only love for Tanya and hatred for himself there. Andy pushed Ashu away and started to leave but then he suddenly stopped and turned back.

'Where is she though?' he asked. 'Is she in trouble?'

'If she's not with you, how can she be in trouble?' Ashu said defiantly.

Andy shook his head in frustration and thought for a while. Then he left that place with his boys.

Ashu was lying by the roadside. It was 6:30 pm. He was hurt and bleeding. He managed to stand up finally and noticed that daylight was fading. He had to manage tonight and he had to find her. He started walking, searching for a bus stand.

Chapter 25

After walking for almost fifteen minutes, he found a place, a charitable house, a place where one could not get facilities like we do in a hotel but could still get a place to stay at relatively cheaper rates and sometimes even free of cost. We could also get some medicines. That was what he needed right then. He entered that place and asked if he could stay. They asked about his condition. He again lied and convinced them.

They treated him and gave him some healthy soup. They also provided him with a bed. He rested for half an hour, but images of everything that had happened lately started haunting him.

He immediately opened his eyes. He took out his phone and dialed her number again. Still it was switched off.

He was in a rather helpless position. He was in another state, amongst unknown people, and she was not reachable. He went out and sat down on the stairs. Very few people were on the road. His whole body was hurting.

He decided to call his family. They were very happy to get his call. They were worried about him. He lied again to his family. He told them that he had gone out of station with his friends and lost his mobile phone. He had just got a new sim activated for his old number. That was why he had not been able to talk.

His family wished him well and asked him to come back soon. He got a little emotional speaking to his mother. But he controlled himself and disconnected the call. He felt relaxed after talking to his family.

Someone came up to him and asked him to come for dinner. He started eating the food, but when he thought about her position, he got up and left.

How is she and where is she?

This thought was killing him, but he had no choice but to wait until next morning. He took his medicine, went to bed, and started thinking again as he closed his eyes.

When he opened his eyes, it was 1 pm. He immediately got up and got ready. He had some tea but was reluctant to eat anything. But a strange man sitting along with him said; 'I saw you come in last night with injuries. Did you get the proper treatment?'

'Yes, I did.'

'Why are you not eating anything?'

'I'm not hungry,'

'If you don't eat, the medicines are not going to help you. You're not going to feel well. And you need to keep your health up. I feel that you have a lot of things to do. If you're going to do them, then you need your strength. You should eat a proper meal.'

The strange man said all this with a smile. He began to leave and then turned around and said; 'Sorry if I said too much. I know you are hurt and will not want any lecture. I have a habit of giving advice if I see anything incorrect or wrong happening in front of me. My wife is fed up of it and that's why she doesn't like me.'

The strange man went away. Ashu thought about what he said and realized that he was right.

We have to live to discharge our responsibilities in life and for that we need to eat properly and take medicines if we are unwell.

Ashu ate something, as the strange man had advised, and took his medicines. Then he left the place at around 3 pm, still unsure of what to do. He searched for a bus stand. Thoughts of her were causing his blood pressure to increase.

I made a mistake leaving her yesterday. She is not with Andy, I'm sure of that. But if she's not with him then what has happened to her? Oh man what a fool I am. I was supposed to take care of her. I always make these mistakes. It shows how irresponsible I am.

He sighed and pulled at his hair. There were few people standing there at the bus stand. They were looking at him as they had never seen a young boy talking to himself on the road. He ignored them and started dialing her number again. Of course the attempt was a failure.

His left side hurt and the pain was gradually worsening. He was anxious, confused, frustrated, and angry.

Anyway, he took a bus and asked for a ticket to the airport. He remembered a statement he'd heard when he'd been a kid.

When you don't see a clear path in front of you, then keep going straight. At least you can come back easily in case of failure then.

He looked outside the window. Houses, farms and mountains were speeding past. He saw people gathering on roads, women working on their fields, kids playing. It all looked beautiful, and amazing. But he only wanted to see the airport. And after half an hour, he finally got there.

He was relieved when he saw the airport. It was a quiet place. Not like the airports in other states which were so crowded and noisy.

He entered the airport and asked someone for flight details, but he was surprised to hear that no flights had gone out of there the past few days as few people ever came here.

Oh God where is she? At least give me a sign that she's okay! He sat down on a chair.

He started looking around. A sweeper was cleaning the place. A few people were standing around. He suddenly noticed a face that seemed familiar. A boy of around his age was going out of the airport.

Who is he? Ashu thought. *I have seen him somewhere but can't remember where.*

The boy left that place. Ashu continued scratching his head. But then he decided to forget about it. He had enough problems. He started searching for something on his mobile, but then he saw the boy again. He seemed to have forgotten something at the ticket counter. Ashu decided to call out to him, compelled by curiosity.

'Hey friend!' he cried.

The boy stopped and turned back. Ashu said; 'I think I know you, but I can't remember where I saw you.'

The boy immediately replied; 'I think we met once. My name is Armaan.'

'Oh yes I remember now. We met you near Chandigarh. We dropped you at the market.'

'Yes,' Armaan smiled. 'Thank you again for that.'

'No problem brother. But why are you here?'

'I wanted to get a ticket to my hometown, but there's nothing for the next few days. What about you? What are you doing here, Ashu?'

'How do you know my name? Did I tell you?'

'Yes, you told me that day. And I don't forget things easily.'

'But you forgot my face a few minutes ago. You saw me and ignored me.'

'I remembered you, but I wasn't sure you remembered me. That's why I didn't talk to you.'

'Oh I see,' Ashu said. They were quiet for a while, but then Ashu asked; 'Are you familiar with this area?'

'To some extent.'

'Good, because I have no clue about it.'

'Then why are you sitting here? Are you planning to fly somewhere?'

'No, I'm looking for someone.'

'You had a girl with you. Where is she?'

Ashu asked him if they could go out and talk. Armaan agreed.

'Actually, we had an accident,' Ashu said. He told Armaan that they'd had an accident and then separated from each other due to some unavoidable circumstances. He did not say anything about the police or other issues. Armaan listened to him very carefully and thought for a while.

'If she's not reachable, then there may be several reasons for it,' Armaan said. 'I mean I believe she's fine, but you should consider them all.'

'What are the reasons and what are the options I have?' Ashu asked.

'Did you check all the clinics and hospitals around this place? Because it's possible she's hurt and getting treated in one of them...'

Ashu seemed nervous at the thought.

'Don't be nervous,' Armaan said. 'I'm just asking you to check all options. Think sensibly. If was fit, she would have come here and called you, right?'

He had a point, Ashu realized.

'Where are you staying now?'

'Nowhere really.'

'I will arrange a place for you tonight,' Armaan said. 'And tomorrow you should start searching all the hospitals and clinics. I'll guide you. No problem.'

Armaan took Ashu on his bike and arranged a room for him for the night. They exchanged numbers so that they could contact each other.

'Thank you so much Armaan. I can never thank you enough. You are an angel.'

'No problem my friend,' Armaan said. 'I hope you find her soon. Call me if you need anything. I'm staying here with my friend's family.'

'Sure. Take care.'

Armaan left.

It was almost 7 pm by now. Ashu felt relaxed as he had found someone to guide him. He ordered tea and some bread so that he could take his medicines. He took his medicines and then rested for some time

His journey with Tanya had given him a lot of pain and problems in life, but one thing which he had gained was change. And that's a requirement of every human being in life. He'd adopted these changes very gracefully and that was an achievement for him.

I think I should give Armaan a call as I'm not aware about tomorrow's plan, he thought.

He called, but did not get a reply even after two or three attempts.

Ashu figured that he was busy and would call back.

After some time, he got a call from an unknown number. He picked up the call. It was Armaan.

'Hey Ashu, are you okay? I saw some missed calls from your mobile, but I couldn't pick up. And now my battery is gone. So I'm calling you from a local number.'

'No. problem,' Ashu said. 'I was just wondering where to meet tomorrow.'

'Don't worry. Relax. I'll call you at noon.'

'Okay. I'll wait for your call.'

'Sure. Are you all right?'

'Yep, I'm fine.'

'Okay. Take care. See you tomorrow.'

Ashu disconnected and took a deep breath. He felt relaxed because now tomorrow's plan was confirmed. Even though things were messy, a glimmer of hope made him feel relaxed.

Life without hope is as useless as eyes without dreams. Hope gives us the inspiration to live through tough times. Even when hope proves to be fake, we still do not let go of it. In fact we should never let go of it.

That's how he was behaving now. Armaan had given him hope and he now started feeling relaxed.

He had dinner at around 9 pm. However, as he started eating the food, a memory of Tanya overwhelmed him and he put his plate aside and stood up. He opened the window and took a few breaths of fresh air.

'Oh God...'

He wanted to say something to God, but stopped himself and shook his head. God it seemed was fed up of hearing the same thing from him.

He looked out the window without blinking.

Look at my condition without you. I've completely lost my way after I lost you. I'm not able to find you. I hope you're trying to find me. Maybe I'll find you yet. I hope I do ...

He closed his eyes and a few tears seeped again through his closed eyelids. However, he felt a little more positive now as he was near the airport. Armaan could help him getting out of here and could guide him.

The next day, he started searching for the hospitals and clinics nearby as soon as he woke up, but he could not find anything until evening. He left the hotel with Armaan, but soon realized that Armaan had left him alone. He saw some familiar faces over the course of his search, people who stayed around the place he lived in Delhi. Then he was surprised to see Andy walking towards him, but he did not talk to him.

Somebody touched his back. He turned and surprised to see his parents and roommate. But then everything went dark. He was standing alone now in the dark night with nobody around him. Not one single thing was moving. There was complete silence.

He felt scared and started running away from that dark place very fast. Soon a bus came in front of him and the light of the bus blinded him for a moment. He screamed – and opened his eyes… He was sitting on his bed…

'Oh it was a dream again,' he said to himself. 'A bad and meaningless one.' He started laughing

Anyway, it was 7 am by now. He was sweating and thirsty. He had some water slept again.

He again woke up at around 9:30 am. He immediately took a bath and asked for some tea and sandwiches.

A boy came with tea and started cleaning the room. Ashu was continuously observing him. His clothes were dirty and torn. 'Why are your cloths shabby? Did you fight with someone?'

Ashu asked with a smile.

'No,' the cleaning boy said with a laugh. 'I had a fight with my sister last night and she did it.'

'Why don't you get new clothes?'

'I will, next month. I have no money left this month. I have given everything to my mom.' The boy left the room with that.

'We waste lot of money on parties and other pleasures for no reason and some people wear torn clothes just because they have no money left at the end of the month,' he said to himself and shook his head.

He took a long breath again and stood up to leave. He came out of the hotel and saw that cleaning boy again. He was standing by the side of the road and gazing at the traffic. It was 10.30 am and Armaan had asked to meet at around noon. Ashu smiled and closed his eyes.

He recalled a memory from some months ago, of how Anshu had helped that poor boy in Shimla and taught him a lesson. She made him promise her, and he'd broken his word immediately. Along with her heart and trust...

But now he was changed. And since he had some time on hands, he decided to use it. He called the boy.

'What are you looking at?' Ashu asked.

'Nothing,' the boy said.

Ashu knelt down. 'Actually, I am new here and don't know the way to the market. So can you guide me?' He asked politely and the boy could not deny him.

They went to the market. He asked the poor boy about his family. He had no father, his mother was working as a servant in houses, and his elder brother was working in another hotel. He belonged to a very poor family.

When they reached the market, Ashu kissed the boy's head and gave him a hug. He offered him some money, which he denied. Ashu knew what to do now. He smiled and asked; 'Okay, if you don't want money, then I'll get you something. You'll have to take it because you helped me get here.'

The boy agreed and Ashu took him to a shop and bought him some clothes. The boy thanked him. Ashu hugged him again and said; 'God bless you, and stay happy.'

Ashu watched him go with a smile. He was happy.

Yes Anshu, you're right. It feels good… Really, it feels good…

Chapter 26

He called Armaan without success. After some time, Armaan called back.

'I'm really sorry,' he said. 'There's some issue with my mobile. Where are you?'

'I'm not in the hotel. I'm in the market. When are you coming?'

'I'll be there in an hour. Get back to the hotel and stay there because my mobile is not working.'

Ashu disconnected the phone, started walking towards the hotel again, and reached there soon – and saw some police vans parked in front of the hotel.

He saw the cleaning boy coming towards him. 'What's going on?' he asked.

'They are searching for you and asking about you,' the boy said. 'According to them you've killed people for money. Is it true?'

Ashu did not say anything.

'You need to leave this place soon,' the boy said. 'Otherwise they'll take you with them.'

'Do me a favor,' Ashu told the boy. 'A young boy will come here asking about me. If possible, tell him to call me. Don't take any risks. If it's possible, then do it.' He caressed the boy's face and turned to leave.

'I told them you're a good man,' the boy said.

Ashu smiled and ran away from that place. After some time, he got a call from Armaan. 'Where are you Ashu? I'm at the hotel waiting for you.'

'But Armaan,' Ashu said, 'there are...' He couldn't complete his sentence.

'Are you okay?' Armaan asked. 'I'm waiting at the hotel. Please come here as soon as possible.'

Ashu thought about it. Should he go there or not? And why was Armaan calling him to the hotel? Couldn't he see that there was a lot of trouble out there?

But then again Armaan did not know about his problems.

And he was the only person who could help him.

So Ashu decided to take the risk. He was about to reach the hotel when his phone vibrated again. It was Armaan calling from an unknown number. 'I'm leaving. I need to go to somewhere urgently.'

'I'm about to reach the hotel just wait for some time.'

'Look Ashu, you are wasting my time,' Armaan yelled. 'I'm here for you. I have no reason to be here.'

'I'm sorry. I'll tell you everything in detail, but give me some time,' Ashu begged.

'I'll wait for another fifteen minutes. It is about Tanya. You know Andy is after you guys. Are you getting what I'm trying to say?' Armaan asked.

'Yes. Please wait for some time. I'm about to reach the hotel.'

He neared the hotel and noticed that the cops were still standing there.

How to get past them? He suddenly saw Armaan coming out of the hotel. He started walking down the road. Ashu followed him for some time and then called; 'Hey Armaan!'

Armaan turned back. He looked bewildered. 'Where were you? I was anxious about you.'

'The cops were there so I didn't want to take a risk.'

'I understand.'

'We need to leave this place. Then we can talk in detail.'

'Sure buddy,' Armaan said. They started walking down the road.

'Sorry I made you angry,' Ashu said, 'But I was…'

'I was not angry. But I need to leave this place tomorrow for some personal reasons. That's why I got annoyed.'

'Where are you going?'

'Just going to meet one of my relatives. That's why I wanted to do everything I can for you today itself.'

'Thanks buddy,' Ashu said. They both smiled at each other.

'Is your phone okay now?' Ashu asked.

'Yes, it's working better now. But I think it's getting old. Like me.' They both laughed.

'So,' Armaan said, 'the plan is to search for Tanya in the nearest clinics and hospitals.'

'But where do we begin?'

Armaan was about to answer when his phone rang. He excused himself and walked a little distance away to take the call. He took a while to finish. He disconnected and came back.

'What happened? You look worried,' Ashu said.

'Nothing,' Armaan said. 'I'll tell you what to do and then I need to leave. I'll see you after some time, but my phone will be available so don't worry.'

He told Ashu what to do and then took a bus from there.

Ashu bent down to pick up a paper slip that had fallen down from Armaan's pocket. He read it and thought for a while. Then he got onto a bus, stood near the driver's seat, and made a call.

In the other bus, Armaan was sitting with his closed eyes. He got a call. He saw that it was from Ashu's mobile. He took a very long breath, but did not take the call. After some time his phone vibrated again, but this time he picked up. He said politely; 'Yes boss, you stay there for some time with him. I'm about to get there… No, I didn't meet him. You don't worry and take care.'

He disconnected and immediately got another call. Now he talked authoritatively.

'Yes, I'm going to the Airport and luckily there is a flight today. We will reach there by nightfall. Now don't call again and again, I will tell you once I'm there.' He started listening and then suddenly yelled; 'I'm not joking here. She was unconscious in the night. That's why her phone was switched off. And it will remain switched off until we get there. Don't worry. Once we get there, I will leave her with you so that you can ask her as many as question you like. Now don't call again. If needed, I'll contact you.' He hung up.

Soon the bus reached the airport. He stepped out of the bus and started walking towards the airport. He noticed that someone was following him. He turned around and was shocked to see Ashu, standing there. He was smiling.

'You missed something there,' Ashu said. 'Check your right pocket.'

Armaan did not say anything.

'You forgot Andy's address when you left me today,' Ashu said. 'Don't worry. I got it for you.'

And with that he spanked Armaan's face. Armaan fell down.

Actually, his suspicions had been aroused when Armaan had told him that morning; 'Andy is after you guys.'

But he had never ever told Armaan about Andy. Andy was a different chapter altogether.

He had also been confused as to how police had discovered his location that morning. Only he and Armaan knew about it.

And thirdly, Armaan had never once called him from his own mobile. Every time he had given an excuse.

And when Ashu had told him he could not come to hotel because of the cops, he had said he understood. But how could he? He did not know about Ashu's problems with the police.

All of this had troubled him that morning. And when Armaan had taken his phone out from his pocket, a paper slip had fallen out of it. Ashu had been shocked to see Andy's address on that paper slip.

Now he was sure about Armaan being Andy's man. He was the one who had been following them right from the beginning. A few days ago, when Armaan had taken a lift from them to the market, that had been no coincidence. It had been planned.

Now it was clear to Ashu that Andy had trapped both of them. Armaan was working for Andy and the one who had informed the police every time. Ashu had trusted him and he'd been betrayed. *He must also have Tanya.*

Now everything was clear to him. Ashu pulled Armaan up by his collar. 'Where is she? I'll leave you because I know Andy sent you to follow us, but tell me about her.'

Armaan did not reply. Ashu slapped his face again. It was not as brutal as the previous one, but it still hurt him. Armaan fell down again and Ashu pulled him up again by the collar.

'You betrayed me, buddy,' Ashu said and slapped his face again. This time, he lost control of his emotions and tears poured out of his eyes. He wiped his eyes and asked; 'Why did you betray me? Did I ever do anything wrong to you? Did I do anything wrong? Did I?'

He let Armaan go and turned away. He looked up and sighed.

Oh God, this is not fair... Not this time... It was my mistake. Why did you give her pain? That's not fair at all. Those were my sins...

He shook his head with frustration. He had understood that the execration of Anshu had hit him now – and Tanya was caught in it for no reason.

He turned around again angrily, to kick Armaan, but this time Armaan was ready and he fought back. Ashu fell down. As he tried to recover himself, Armaan kicked him again.

Armaan wanted to hit him again, but stopped. Ashu was ready now and hit Armaan on his knee. Armaan lost his balance completely and fell down. Ashu landed two or three hard punches on Armaan's chest. Armaan tried to escape, but could not succeed. Blood was continuously dripping out of his mouth. But he was laughing that surprised Ashu.

'Why are you hitting me like this?' Armaan asked. 'I'm a strong man. Please just kill me. I know I've committed a sin.'

'You betrayed me. For money.'

Armaan laughed. 'Do you really think I did it for money and that I'm Andy's man? No, I am not. I don't even know where he stays. That is why you found his address in my pocket. And do you really think I kidnapped her at Andy's request? No man. I could never ever do that. Yes, I'm the one who told the cops where you were. And yes, I've been following you since you left Delhi.

'And here's something you don't know: I killed those two people. You started it and I finished it. I killed them and you know what the problem is? Fortunately for me and unfortunately for you, I own a red car too. After you pushed them out of your car and left that place. The eyewitness couldn't see my face and just saw a young guy alone in a red car.'

Ashu was shocked. He still could not understand the 'why' though. Why had he followed them from Delhi if he'd not been Andy's man? Why kill those two men? Ashu was about to ask when Armaan's phone started ringing.

'Someone wants to talk to you badly,' Ashu observed.

'My girlfriend,' Armaan said.

'Talk to her. Because I'm not letting you go. The police want me for two murders and I won't mind if they hang me for three.'

The behavior of Armaan was very odd. Ashu had hurt him, but he was still laughing.

The two of them were staring into each other's eyes like beasts. Armaan's phone was still ringing. He looked into the distance, looked behind Ashu, and started laughing even louder. Ashu turned to look back. He pushed Armaan away. Now they both fell down. Ashu was surprised to see someone coming their way. It was a girl.

Ashu kept his eyes on her. Another boy was following her. As she came closer, he was stunned to see her face.

It was Tanya, walking towards them.

Ashu assumed that Andy had sent Armaan to follow them and bring Tanya back to him by any means necessary. And that they had managed to grab her when Ashu had left Tanya alone in the bus.

He thought now, that she had got a chance, escaped from their clutches, and come back to him

He thought his love story was going smoothly. He'd had some issues, troubles and fear, but then love is not proven true until it faces all these challenges.

He imagined that his love could triumph over all odds. After all, that was what he'd heard since childhood and read everywhere.

But he had forgotten one thing. What about the things he left incomplete? Who would complete them?

However, his love story was not as smooth as he thought.

How deluded he was...

As she came closer, he started gazing at her face. He smiled, but she seemed to be tense. Her focus was not on him. She was looking beyond him

She walked past him and went to Armaan.

Yes...

Armaan. Her Boyfriend...Her Partner...Her Love... For years...

Their love story had begun around seven years ago, in a college of Delhi University and grew on the roads of Delhi. Armaan belonged to Mohali (which was in Punjab) and she was from Maharashtra.

Armaan was a shy person, but he was very serious about his relation with her. He could do anything for her – including killing two people.

On the other hand, Tanya was very open-minded. She was a flirt with uncontrollable feelings in her heart. But since he had never caught her red handed, her relation with him remained clean. Her major problem was that she had no control over her feelings, and that was why she'd had several affairs. But she never left him, despite these numerous flings.

Anyway, she held Armaan's hand now. She knelt down and took him in her arms.

'Are you sure you're holding the right guy?' Armaan asked.

'Shut up. Stop blabbering.' She slapped his face gently. Her eyes were teary.

'No, I'm serious. Because the boy who's lying next to me is claiming that you're his girlfriend and that you love him. I don't like this. I think I will kill him.' He laughed again.

'No, you don't need to do anything sweetheart,' Tanya said and hugged him tightly. She helped him up

Ashu was watching all this drama unfold, but he was confused by the scene even though everything was clear. He was behind her. She wiped blood off Armaan's face. She turned back angrily.

Her eyes and Ashu's met. She took a long breath. She knew that the time had come now to have another breakup. However, this time, she was not feeling comfortable because Armaan was standing in front of them.

'Tanya… Baby…' Ashu said. 'What is all this?'

He came close to her and tried to touch her face, but she did not allow him to. She yelled; 'What have you done? How dare you touch him?'

The man who had been following her was Armaan's childhood friend, Achal. He helped Armaan up. He took Armaan away from that place and sat him down somewhere where he could rest.

Now Tanya and Ashu were alone.

'Are you happy now that you hurt him?' Tanya asked.

'Tanya, baby,' Ashu said, 'I'm not in a position to endure all this and –'

'What about me? There's nothing between us and don't call me baby. I'm not your baby.'

'What?'

'Yes.' She stepped away from him.

'Are you mad? You are saying there's nothing between us? The time we spent together? The issues we faced together? Does it all mean nothing to you?'

She got depressed now. She took a long breath again and put a hand on her forehead. She was breathing very fast and looking around but not into his eyes.

'Look at me,' Ashu said.

'Look Ashu, there is some confusion,' she said in a low voice.

'What confusion?'

'Listen to me, please. This is complicated. I Love Armaan and we have been in a relation for the last seven years. We want to settle down together. So I request you to please go away from here. Please, I'm begging you.' She was looking into his eyes now.

He now started to understand. He had been duped badly. She had used him intentionally to satisfy her needs. He was quiet for some time. He sighed and suddenly his eyes started getting wet.

'Ashu please,' Tanya said. 'Don't do this. Be mature.'

'Don't play with me,' Ashu said. 'I thought a lot for you. I thought a lot for us, gave you every single second of my life, thought about you and you only, day and night. I trusted you and our relation. Your relation has changed me and given me the strength to change things. I changed myself for you. I was not with you to just enjoy my time, but to make you happy and feel safe.'

'Ashu, we knew each other only for a few weeks.'

'How does that matter?'

'I've been in a relationship with Armaan for seven years!'

'Then why did you start things with me?' he roared.

'Look Ashu, don't create scene here. I've to leave now.'

She turned to leave but he pulled her around and yelled; 'Who do you think you are to just come into my life and then leave it when you feel like it?'

He raised his hand to slap her, but controlled his anger. It was enough to make Armaan angry though. He roared from where he was; 'Don't even try touching her shadow!' He tried to come over, but she stopped him.

'Armaan,' Tanya said, 'Please…please…please… You stay away from all this and rest.'

'But why are you listening to him now?' Armaan demanded. 'You said we needed him until we got out of this mess. We're out now. Let's go,'

Ashu got angry. He tried to hit Armaan, but Tanya came in between them.

'Stop this,' Tanya said. 'Ashu, please leave now. And Armaan, stop this if you love me.'

'Ashu, you are a dead man,' Armaan said. 'I've just informed the cops that you are here and they'll be here soon.'

'Armaan, you promised me,' Tanya said. 'This is not fair at all.' She held his hand and took him back to where he had been sitting before. She came back to Ashu then.

'Ashu look,' she said, 'it would be better for you if you left this place soon. Otherwise you will be in trouble.'

Ashu begged; 'Tanya, please don't do this. I've done a lot to come here; only you are my strength now. We were together for millions of seconds, felt each other everywhere. How could you be so cruel? Don't leave my hand because I love you straight from the heart and I think about you every second. I cannot even think of breathing without you. Please don't do this. Please don't.' He was weeping now

'Look Ashu,' Tanya said, 'if you did all this for me then that's your problem. I never asked you to help me or come with me and please don't give me these tears, they hold no value for me. I'm sorry for this and thank you very much for helping me get here.'

'That's all you have to say?'

She ignored that completely. She said; 'Please. I'm telling you for the last time; leave this place or else you will get caught.

And after this, I'm not even going to recognize you. I'm sorry about this. But I want to live my life with Armaan and without any tension. And I can do anything for that. You are a sweet and good boy. I like you, but I don't love you. I am sorry that I lost control over my feelings now and then, but I never loved you.'

As she completed her statement, they heard a police van coming up to them.

Tanya said; 'Look Ashu, I have to leave now. You also run away.'

He was quiet for a few minutes. His eyes were completely wet. She stepped down but he called after her again. She looked back.

Ashu said; 'Tanya, you broke my heart and trust. Somebody told me some time ago that betrayal is murderous – or worse.'

Tanya said; 'It's your mistake if you trusted me. You should've thought a thousand times before trusting me.'

'Tanya, you betrayed me and I will always remember this.'
'Anything else?' She smiled and looked away.

She held Armaan's hand and started walking in the direction of the airport. He was looking at her with sad, wet eyes.

He knelt down and started crying now. Really crying. Not loudly, but the flow of tears was very fast.

He was crying over a girl with whom he'd spent a lot of time. He'd destroyed himself to protect her. He was looking at her with the hope that she would turn back. But it did not happen. She'd made fun of his feelings when she said; 'It's your problem if you trusted me.'

He had lost everything now. He had been accused of killing two people and the only witness to his innocence was Tanya – who had just screwed him badly and left. The police had almost reached that place and now he had no option left but to run.

He stood, turned around, and looked at Tanya. She was walking away from him, holding Armaan's hand. She seemed happy. His eyes were full of fear and tears. He turned around and started to run.

Chapter 27

He kept running and finally reached the place where the road ended and the deep valley began. It was raining. He closed his eyes.

He raised both his hands and started crying. Thunder was crashing in the skies above. He roared like a beast that was hurt badly.

'Why? Why? I was sincere this time. Why did it happen?' He stopped crying, started looking straight, and stood still as a statue for the next five minutes.

Suddenly, he felt as if somebody was standing with him. He turned left and saw Anshu standing with him. But the noise of the thunderstorm distracted him. He looked left again, but nobody was there now. He anxiously looked around that place and kept thinking for a few minutes. His slowly began to laugh with tears in his eyes.

'So, it's revenge? You took trust for trust and rewarded betrayal with betrayal... You made a fair trade with me, my Lord!'

He was talking to God. He was laughing and crying at the same time as it seemed he had finally understood the game of luck. He got it now. He'd played with others' trust so badly that somebody had destroyed his own trust utterly.

Trust is what helps us create relations in life. Every relationship we have in our life takes trust to create. Therefore, trust is the lifeline of every human being. And if it is broken, then it hurts.

The story of Ashu was a game of luck. He had been deceived in the same way he had deceived Anshu.

One month ago, on the 2nd of August, a young boy had broken the trust and heart of a girl. Now this boy was asking God: 'I was sincere this time but why did it happen to me?'

If he was serious, then what could, Anshu, who was actually an innocent, sweet girl at heart say? She had been more than serious about a stupid and unreliable boy.

And this boy now found himself in the same situation which he had left that innocent, pretty girl in one month ago.

So what had happened to her after he'd walked out of her life?

Anshu's situation one month ago

Anshu had told Ashu;

'I am not accepting your apology now. I will accept it on the day you actually feel sorry from your heart and feel the same pain that I am feeling today. And on that day you will cry like I am crying now.'

He had left her saying 'Anything else?' and given her the same expression that Tanya would end up giving him.

He ignored Anshu when she was crying for him and, in return, Tanya would ignore him when he was crying for her.

Anshu fell down as he left Sakshi's place and the same would happen with him when Tanya left him. But Manya and Sakshi had been there with Anshu to support her. When he fell down though, nobody was there to support him. That was his bad luck. Both Tanya and Ashu played with the trust of others for their own desires and needs.

One used it to satisfy his lust and amuse himself while the other used it to fulfill her needs and to satisfy her uncontrollable desires.

They reduced trust to disgusting, shameful, and cheap thing. And they didn't care.

Anshu was innocent as she had never ever played with the feelings of others. So the damage that she'd taken was the worst.

In his case, the score was settled. He broke someone's trust once and so someone broke his trust in return.

He asked God 'Why?' and he got his answer immediately.

It was an execration that came from Anshu's heart.

He understood everything.

But was it really Anshu, who'd execrated him? Or was it something else?

Present Day

He understood everything now. Why it had all happened to him, why he was crying, why he was alone, and why his trust and heart were broken.

An execration from my ex-girlfriend…

Depression, frustration, and physical damage had already crushed him completely. He was standing at the entrance of a deep valley.

He suddenly raised both of his arms and closed his eyes. He was quiet for few minutes and then suddenly screamed; 'I'm sorry Anshu! Please forgive me. I'm sorry! Really sorry!'

He lost control of his emotions again. He heard a noise. He opened his eyes and looked around him. He smiled. 'You also betray me now. You promised me that when I'd feel the same pain you did, you would come to me. But you're not here. Maybe you're still too angry.'

He wiped his eyes and sat there with his head bowed. It was almost night. He continued sitting there for almost half an hour. Long curly hairs were covering his forehead and falling over his eyes. His bearded face had lost all its cuteness.

Suddenly, he saw a police van coming in his direction. He started walking down the road. His wet eyes were full of fear. He tried to hide his face but, fortunately, the van was not following him.

Soon he reached a bus stand and got a bus that was going down into the valleys.

Where to go and what to do?

However he had no answer to this question. There were few people sitting in the bus and, at one point, the driver asked everyone to get out as it was the last stand. They all got down.

He again sat down by the side of the road to rest. Suddenly he heard the noise of bells. He saw a temple, very near that place. He started thinking about something that he'd always heard his parents and grandparents say.

'If you are ever restless and sad in life then only one place can solve your issues,' and that place was in front of him now… A temple.

He was not used to all this, but he did not think twice and stepped into the temple. He sat in front of the idol with both his head and shoulders down. He closed his eyes to meditate, but could not do so as all the events that had happened started coming back to him. He opened his eyes and started looking at the statue of God. He kept looking for the next fifteen minutes. This gave him some peace as he was concentrating on the eyes of God and not on the events that he had faced today.

He slowly closed his eyes and fell asleep.

He suddenly opened his eyes. Somebody was asking him to get up. 'Where do you live?' he was asking.

'Actually, I…' Ashu could not say anything. He came out of the temple and sat down on the steps.

The priest of the temple came out and asked him; 'Why are you not leaving this place?'

He told the priest some made-up story and managed to spend the night at the temple. The entire night, he was haunted by nightmares of everything he'd faced of late. The entire night, Tanya's face and attitude disturbed him.

But, perhaps because of the aura of the temple, he finally managed to fall asleep.

Chapter 28

He opened his eyes in the early morning. Since he was in the temple, he had to get up. The man at the temple asked him to take a bath on the rooftop of the temple. He felt fresh after taking his bath. He then took a part in the morning prayer and ate some fruits for breakfast. The priest was very kind to him. He completed everything and left the temple on a good note.

His mood was not as bad as it had been last night. But the reality hit him eventually. He had lost everything. The cops were after him for killing two people. He switched on his phone, but did not get anything. He thought Tanya would message him, but she did not do so. He continued walking and sitting along the roadside for no reason. He started feeling a sharp pain in his heart.

'You did wrong Tanya. We were enjoying our time together even in the worst scenarios.'

He let his male ego go now and started crying like a little girl. He could not spend all his nights in a temple. That would not work forever. He again started feeling depressed.

What has happened to me? I used to be such a fun-loving person. One girl trapped me. And I was such a fool that I couldn't see her intentions. She was using me right through but I'm still thinking about her. It hurts so much!

He started listening to some music on his phone – by far one of the best things to do in a situation like this. He was now getting more open to create his own things

"Meri Khoyee Aur Beqaabu Nazren Tumhe Dhundhati Hai

Har Jagah Jabse Tum Ho Bichhade

Huye Kyon Judaa Aur Kab Aaogay, Aaogay Bhi Ke Nahi
Yahi Puchati Hai Mujhse Mere Dil Ki Raahen
Me Chal Rahaa Hun Unhi Raaston Pe
Jinpe Hum Chale Thae Kabhi,
Ghurte Hain Mujhko Yeh Nazaare,
Pedh, Phool. Kaanten Aur Log Sabhi
Kahan Ho Tum Sun Lo Mere Dil Ki Sadaa
Yaa Maang Lo Khudaa Se Mere Marne Ki Dua
Kahan Kho Gaye Ho Tum Mere Dil Ka Chain Leke
Aur Mujhko Dard-e-Dil Deke
Meri Aankhen Tumhe Hi Dhundhati Hai Har Jagah,
Aur Dhadkane Tham Si Gayee Hain Yun Bewajah
Ziddi Dil Kar Raha Hai Mujhe Kaabu,
Mere Faisale Ho Rahen Hain Mujhse Beqaabu
Kahan Ho Tum Sun Lo Mere Dil Ki Sadaa
Yaa Maang Lo Khudaa Se Mere Marne Ki Dua
Ik Baat Bataao Kya Paaya Tumne Mujhe Iss Kadar
Rulaake,
Tanha Karke Aur Mere Iss Dil Ko Dukhake
Ab Rah Nahi Paaye Yeh Tere Bin Ae Bekhabar,
Aake Cheer De Is Dil Ko Aur Fir Le Iski Khabar
Ik Baari Aao Yun Na Sataayo,
Jaan Chali Jaayegi Saanson Ki Lehron Pe Milke Toh Dikhao
Kahan Ho Tum Sun Lo Mere Dil Ki Sadaa
Yaa Maang Lo Khudaa Se Mere Marne Ki Dua"
(My Lost and uncontrolled eyes are finding you
Everywhere from the time we split
Why we split up and when you'll come back, whether you'll
come or not
That's what I ask from my soul

I'm still walking on the same road where we walked together
Everything around are staring at me
Where are you, Please listen to my sigh
Else, pray for my destruction
I don't know where you lost
After taking piece of my mind
And giving a pain to my feelings
My eyes finding you all the time everywhere and
My heart has stopped beating without you.
My Stubborn heart has controlled my mind completely and
Now my decisions are not in my control
Where are you, Please listen to my sigh
Else, pray for my destruction
Tell me what you got when you made me cry and desolated
Your memories pinch me like thorn
Now I am not able to live without you
Please come back, slit my heart, and then take care of it
Please come once, don't ail me like this and meet
Otherwise, I'll annihilate myself
Where are you, Please listen to my sigh
Else, pray for my destruction)

He kept wiping his eyes. He stopped weeping and calmed down. He now kept looking in front and seemed to be deep in thought. Now his expression started changing and, suddenly, he slapped his own face three times.

Why? Why? Why? He shook his head, eyes wet.

Why did I trust her and believe her?

After some time, he sniffed and wiped his eyes. Now the time had come to take a decision about the problems he was facing. Otherwise surviving was going to be difficult for him in the coming days. But he could not accept what had happened to him.

We normally do not accept what we get unexpectedly. Now Ashu was a victim of Emotional Persecution. He'd got from Tanya what he'd given Ashu.

The day drew on. He saw the temple where he had spent last night in a good mood. It was not very far away from where he was. He decided to go there again to calm his mind down. Even temporary peace would work right now.

He reached the temple again and as soon as he entered, he started feeling peace. The evening prayer was about to start. This was the first time in his life that he was present for both the morning and evening prayers. He tried to meditate during the prayer. After the prayer, he came out, sat on the stairs, and started gazing at the people going out.

This is actually a place where people come in with their problems and go out with hope in their minds and a smile on their lips. That's why this place is considered so sacred. He was an idiot to lie yesterday to be able to spend the night here.

He had told the priest that he'd had a fight with his family and had been thrown out of his home last night.

He was feeling ashamed of his behavior now. After some time, the Priest came to have a look around the temple. He again noticed Ashu sitting there. He put his hand on his head.

'Hey child,' the priest said. 'It seems that things are not yet settled in your life.'

'Yes, I mean...' Ashu could not say anything. He held the priest's hand and asked him to sit. He did not explain his exact position but gave the priest a general idea.

'I'm sorry,' Ashu said. 'I know it's a sin, but still... I'm really sorry.'

'No problem,' the priest smiled. 'I knew you were telling lie.'

'Then why did you allow me to stay?' Ashu asked.

'You seemed to need some mental relaxation,' the priest smiled. But he added;

'Always keep one thing in mind though. This place doesn't give solutions to your problems. It only helps you regain the mental strength that was lost because of some adverse event that happened in your life. Only mental strength and nothing else. Then you can work on your problems with a strong and fresh mind as only you can solve your issues. And one more thing, this place doesn't give any strength to your heart because the only thing that can do that is the company of the people who are in your heart.'

'I've lost my way completely,' Ashu said sadly.

'Look child,' the priest said, 'the night doesn't come when we close our eyes and the day doesn't come when we turn on the lights. They come when nature intends them to.'

Ashu didn't understand.

The priest explained; 'Okay, if you don't get the answer to your current problem, then reevaluate your problem in detail and try to find the source of your problem. Once you get that, you will get the answers to all the questions you have related to your current problem. People usually forget the source of their problems and waste their entire lives searching here and there for answers. Sometimes, we ignore the source intentionally just because we do not want to see it. That is our dilemma and the root cause of all our tensions.'

'What if the source is a person who is gone from our life?'

'Have the guts to confront them and ask for a second chance. If somebody actually has true feelings for you, then he or she will accept you irrespective of your mistake. But this can happen only once in a relation. Not repeatedly.'

Ashu started laughing

'Why are you laughing?'

'I always thought we got solutions at temples, not lectures. I'm sorry, but...'

Now the priest started laughing loudly too.

'For smart people, the mere wag of a finger is enough and, for someone who is stupid, even surrendering your entire body may not enough. They'll go away saying that it didn't work because we hid our shadows from them. And as far as this sacred place is concerned, this is not a shop where you get things. People commit sins and then come here to repent. They think all their sins are washed away with that. They talk to God, confess their mistakes. But they don't have the guts to face the victim of their sins. It is like this: you damage the life of X and apologize in front of Y. That's stupid. We are all made up of the same divine substance that runs through this whole universe. So try to look inside yourself. You will find the entire universe inside if you have the guts to see it. And now I think you need to work on solving your own issue.' The priest again put his hand on Ashu's head. He smiled and took a very long breath.

Ashu said; 'I believe I need tonight to think over my issues, but I won't stay here because I have got some mental peace now... I think.'

He smiled and took leave of the priest. He had again got a lecture but now he was not pissed off by that. He left that sacred place and arranged for another place to spend the night.

That night, he talked to his family and assured them that he'd be back home in two or three days. He seemed happy. He ate dinner and then went outside for a walk. But then his mind went back to Tanya.

Why did Tanya do this to me?

As the priest had mentioned, he'd got temporary peace of mind but no peace of heart. Whatever therapy he took would never work. He remembered the golden words of the priest. He had to find and reach the source of all his tensions. He started thinking.

I enjoyed many relationships, but the one which I had with her was the longest one. I had many girls, but nobody treated me like her. She kept watch over me and even in the end, she asked me to come back. She slapped me, but it didn't touch my ego. I came in touch with Tanya because I wanted someone who could give me mental relaxation since Anshu's behavior was not letting me live my life peacefully. I felt her presence many times around me. I remember her all the time. I always talked about her, and tried different ways to forget her. But, every time, I kept brining her name up again. Tanya was one of the ways I tried to avoid her. She slapped my face four or five times, but mentally she slaps me on a daily basis. Of course I thought for Tanya more than I ever thought for any other girl and I always wanted to settle down with her, but she never loved me. She used me and sucked everything out of my life. She is the only witness to my innocence, but she still left me alone in this valley with all these problems. So, at this point of time, if I am to think from the heart, then it seems to me that she is my only hope… Yes… Anshu is the source. I have to reach her at any cost. Only she can bring peace to my heart.

He thought for a long time about the source of his problems and the solution was singular: *Anshu.*

He went back to his room and sprawled on the bed.

She loves me and will definitely forgive me if I confront her properly.

That was the last thing he thought before closing his eyes.

Chapter 29

The next morning, he did not waste much time and completed everything very soon. He had quite a few issues to face. There was the police, he did not have much money left, he was physically not fit, and mentally unstable. But he had one hope still motivating him to act – Anshu, his ex-girlfriend.

There was no harm in trying to find out whether Anshu was still willing to endure him or not.

There is always a hope to live for until we die, he thought and smiled.

He took a bus to Chandigarh and thought about dialing Anshu's number. But he mistakenly dialed Tanya – whose phone was switched off. He again felt sad. He deleted her number and started looking out the window. On this same road, he had been enjoying his time with Tanya only some time ago, but now he was all alone.

He was gazing outside and then suddenly he was smiling.

I should've understood that she's a girlfriend. And a girlfriend is a unique character in this universe...

She is possessive in relationship,

She is persuasive while making a decision

She is egoistic when we remonstrate

She puts on a mask of fake self-respect when we mistakenly mistreat her

She is irritating while shopping

She is a liar when it comes to her past relations

She is prodigal about her stuff

She is skimpy about our stuff

She is jealous when we laugh with girls

She is open minded when she clasps hands with other boys

She is innocent when we break up

She is ignorant when she breaks up

But

She gives pleasure when happy

She gives love when happy

She gives physical intimacy when happy

She gives relaxation when happy

She gives peace when happy

She gives comfort when happy

She gives everything when happy basically. Therefore, the one and only way to enjoy everything in life was to make her happy as she was one among the three relations in the life of a male that never got irritated no matter what. These three relations were Mom, Girlfriend, and Daughter.

He was smiling and thinking as the bus reached Chandigarh. He had started thinking positively now as he had already accepted his negatives and started counting the positives of his partner, or rather his ex- partner.

He got out as soon as the bus reached Chandigarh. He still had a smile on his lips.

I'm coming now and won't leave you even if you spurn me…

He got another bus and, within few hours, he reached Delhi. He called his roommate, but got no answer. He got a call from an unknown number a little later.

It was him roommate. 'Hey Ashu. Is everything fine? The police came here, searching for you. I was not here so they asked the neighbors about us. They were searching for you specifically.'

'What did they ask?' Ashu asked.

'I don't know, but they were looking for you.'

'Okay. I'll be back soon.'

He hung up, more worried than ever now.

He got another call. This time it was from his family. He was shocked to learn that the police had visited his home in Punjab and asked his parents about him. His father ordered him to come back home. Ashu assured him that he would be back the next day. He hung up, put a hand on his head and started pulling his hair.

I don't know why people try to change their own lives. I was on an easy path and my life was heaven. But ever since I changed myself and took the correct path, my life has become hell. Anshu told me once that betrayal is murderous or worse. I have to agree. When will this end? Oh God, I am done. I can't endure this anymore. I'm hurt and now my family is also getting hurt by my acts. I'm good for nothing. Please, enough…'

The bus entered in Delhi.

How will I face her? He wondered.

He decided to call her first. He looked nervous while dialing her number. He was sweating. But the number was switched off. He tried again, but with no success. He sent a message; 'Please call me. Please, it's a request.'

Oh God, this is not happening to me. Please Anshu, switch on your phone.

He got out of the bus and took an auto rickshaw to her house. By now it was 5 pm. He dialed her number again, but in vain again. Then he decided to call Manya. Her phone rang, but she did not pick up. He sent her a message, the same message he sent Anshu, and started waiting anxiously for her reply.

'Come on, Manya. Pick up, damn it.'

The auto driver was observing him continuously. He looked back and asked him what happened.

'You'd better look in front and concentrate on driving,' Ashu yelled at him.

The driver did as he was told. Ashu suddenly got a message from Manya. 'Please don't call or send anything. It's a request.' He called again, but she disconnected this time. He again sent a message to her. 'Please, I need to talk to her urgently. I know I don't deserve it, but I still want to talk. I'm calling her continuously, but her number is switched off. Please tell her that I'm calling.'

He got a reply soon. 'Please don't joke. I'm begging you. Please don't disturb us.'

'Please. I wanna meet her once... I beg you... Please, please...'

He did not get a reply for some time. He sent a message again. 'Please?'

After a few minutes, he got a reply

'Okay,' Manya said. 'You wanna meet her? I'm sending you an address... Be there now.' He was shocked to see that it was the address of a hospital. He asked the driver to take him there.

It started to rain. He reached the hospital, left the auto, and started walking. The auto driver called after him; 'Hello! You didn't pay the fare.'

He turned back, paid the auto man, and apologized.

He was standing in front of the hospital and called Manya, but she did not pick up. He sent her a message; 'I'm in front of the hospital. Please tell me where to come?'

'Wait there for five minutes. I'm coming.'

He started waiting. *Please God, let her be all right. I'm begging you. You have already given me lot of pain. She's innocent. Why must she suffer?*

He saw Manya coming his way. She came near him.

He was looking bad. Old shabby clothes. Bearded face. He was looking like an old man. He had wounds on his face and arms. She was looking restless. They were quiet for some time.

'Why are you here?' she asked quietly.

'I…' he could not say anything. He could not even look at her.

'Do you wanna say anything or shall I go back inside?'

'How is she?' he asked anxiously

'Who?'

'Manya please. You know who. Anshu.'

'Don't say her name. Aren't you ashamed to say her name?'

'Please tell me how she is.'

She pointed at him. 'Mark my words. I'll slap you if you ask about her again.' She turned to leave, but he grabbed her arm.

She turned around and slapped his face. It started raining very heavily now. The traffic around was also very noisy. They talked for almost half an hour. Most of the time, she was talking. Once or twice, he said something. His head was bowed. He wanted to get inside the hospital but she would not let him.

He listened to her. He was breathing very fast. She left him alone and went back inside the hospital. He called after her; 'Please Manya! Let me come inside and see her once. I'm begging you.'

He dropped to his knees, but she did not look back. She was crying. He was in shock.

He sat down on the side of the road, head bowed. He was soaked. He kept sitting like that for some time and then, after ten minutes, he looked up angrily with wet eyes. He pulled his hair and then hid his face in his hands.

The rain had stopped and there was silence everywhere. The wind started blowing softly and people were enjoying the weather.

Some people were eating ice creams while others were having coffee or tea. Different people have different priorities...

He was continuously looking at everyone around him, but he was thinking about what she'd told him. He had come here to be sheltered by Anshu, but it seemed that he was not about to get anything but frustration. Manya had denied him his wish to go into the hospital see her.

He stood up and hailed an auto. He reached the bus stand and took a seat in a bus. It seemed he was going back to his hometown. The bus started moving, but he kept thinking about what Manya had told him about Anshu.

He started thinking about her situation and closed his eyes.

Chapter 30

Back to 2nd August

Anshu's condition after that was not good. She went to her room as soon as they reached home. She pretended to be sick and asked everyone to leave her alone. Manya did not say anything to parents but she was disturbed.

'What happened?' she asked Anshu.

'Manya please, I need some rest,' Anshu said.

'But …' Manya couldn't say anything. 'I love you,' she said. She caressed her sister's face and left the room.

As Manya left the room, Anshu hid her face under a pillow and started crying. She was not loud. She controlled herself, but still the pillow cover got completely soaked.

She became a victim of emotional persecution after being misused by Ashu, her boyfriend, her love. Actually, he'd used her badly but smartly.

He had met with her on a rainy day at a college campus and become mesmerized by her beauty. He then threw some magical words at her and she'd caught them. Initially, she'd also taken him lightly, but soon she was trapped in his magic and believed in his fake emotions.

She was a fool then because she'd forgotten one simple thing. How can love be possible at first sight? She had believed a person who'd said he loved her as soon as he'd seen her. She behaved like a lunatic and now she was crying. She was not able to close her eyes because, every time she did, she saw the event that had happened at Sakshi's house.

She was still sprawled on her bed, frequently blinking her tears away. Suddenly, she stood up, took her phone and thought of calling him, but then stopped herself..

'Why did you do this to me Ashu? I was sincere to you. I gave you everything, not because of any lust or passion. But because I loved you so much…I love you so much even now. You know I love you with all my heart… You came in and went away so easily from my life. You know me, I can live without talking to you if you are part of my life, but can't live if you are not a part of my life.'

She was talking to herself. She started walking very fast up and down the room. She relaxed on the bed for a few minutes then again started walking again. She again sat on the bed then and started shifting uncomfortable. She wiped her eyes. There was anger in them now. It seemed there was a devil inside her now, controlling her system.

'Ashu, you didn't do right by me. I always gave you my love and affection and you used me to satisfy your lust and needs. But I won't leave you be.'

She stood up, found a blade in her room, put it against her left arm, and…

Game over…

Present Day (Ashu)

The bus stopped. The driver asked the passengers to eat some food if they wanted. Stoppage time was thirty minutes. Ashu did not come out. He was deep in thought.

I behaved badly that day. She was in pain and I was planning to enjoy my time with other girls. Shame on me…

He looked at his reflection in the glass of the window.

A few weeks ago (Anshu)

Fortunately, her mom came into the room to check if she was all right. They took her to the hospital immediately. She remained unconscious till the next day.

Manya explained everything to parents before she regained consciousness. Her father wanted to talk to Ashu straightaway, but she stopped him because she just wanted to forget the event now. She apologized to her family and then they all came back home. The next day, her parents talked to her about the matter.

'Look Anshu,' her father said, 'what you did was not good. But we understood your point and now we are expecting you to understand ours and put everything behind"

'Okay. I will try.'

'Look child,' her mom said. 'We gave you everything you asked for, but that doesn't mean you can do anything.'

'Mom, please give me some time to recover,' Anshu said. She left the room. Her parents did not like that at all. She had a fight with her parents on the issue. This was a mistake on their part.

They were asking her to leave everything behind and start a new life. They were correct, but the way they asked was incorrect. Also, the timing was wrong. They were expecting her to look at all her responsibilities and accountabilities. That was good, but not at this point of time.

At this point of time, Anshu needed backing. She needed someone who could really let her be free to do anything and keep an eye on her all the time. However, what usually happens in these situations is that people ask the victims of emotional persecution to understand his or her responsibilities towards the family and everything else – which actually lets the victim down.

Lectures work, but not all the time.

She was unhappy with her parent's behavior. They gave her everything, but were lacking the real support she needed at this time. She went outside after two or three days and spent her entire day sitting at metro stations alone and listening to some sad songs, she kept thinking about her time with him.

That's how she was spending her days. Every day she went outside and came back frustrated. Every night, she checked his status on all the social networking tools. Again, a sad and bad day would end as she closed her eyes.

Present Day (Ashu)

The bus stopped again, this time because it had broken down. This time the stoppage time was more than one hour. Ashu felt uncomfortable and came back inside the bus and took his seat again. His eyes were full of sorrow, grief. He needed some rest. He closed his eyes,

A few weeks ago (Anshu)

It was a beautiful day, but the only thought that came to her mind was the time she had spent with Ashu in the mountains.

She'd been suffering from low blood pressure and been complaining to her parents about her health. Her family doctor observed her condition and advised a change of place for some days. They decided to go to Shimla.

'How are you feeling now?' Manya asked when they got there.

'Fine,' Anshu lied, smiling.

They reached the same place where, some months ago, Anshu had come with Ashu. She had mix feelings about being there. She was happy because she was at the very place where, some months ago, she'd spent some beautiful time with her love, but the very next moment she was feeling sad because she was here again and that love was no longer a part of her life.

So same place, same soul, same heart and same love but both negative and positive waves were around that gives an indication that as seasons can change the look of one place drastically, fate also can change the life of a person unexpectedly within the same surroundings.

One night, before going for dinner, they were walking around the market. She was not feeling comfortable on those streets, the same streets where she had done so many wild and crazy things with her former love. She kept her distance from her family and reached a part of the road from where she could look down. She closed her eyes.

Present day (Ashu)

The bus reached Chandigarh at 5 am. He went out and checked his phone. He had received a lot of calls from his family and some messages. He was shocked. One of the messages said that, last night, cops had come to his house and taken his father and uncle to the police station. They'd asked about him. They'd also told his family everything, in detail. He shook his head and sighed.

Such a hound I am; morally and practically reprehensible... He started laughing.

He was laughing for two reasons. One, because of what he had given to his loved ones, be it his family or Anshu. And second because when he checked his pocket, he did not find his wallet. He had lost it somewhere on the bus that had now left that place. He checked his pocket. He had some money, around two thousand five hundred rupees.

He stopped laughing, took a taxi from that place, and started a new journey. He looked out of the taxi that was taking him through all those roads where he had spent some beautiful and thrilling times with Tanya. He opened the window and felt the wind on his face..

A few weeks ago (Anshu)

She opened her eyes as Manya called her from behind. She wiped her eyes.

'What happened?' Manya asked. 'Are you okay? Mom is calling you for dinner?'

'Yeah I'm fine,' Anshu said. She smiled, but her eyes told the truth.

'What are you looking at?'

'Nothing. Just trying to measure the depth of this valley.'

'Why?'

'No reason. Let's eat.' They had some fun over dinner. Both the sisters ate ice-cream even though it was getting very frosty.

Soon, they decided to get back to hotel. It was getting too cold. In the room, they planned for the next day. Lots of shopping, gaming, enjoyment, and eating, was on the list. After a while, they slept. But Anshu thought a lot for about an hour and only then closed her eyes.

Chapter 31

Present day (Ashu)

He opened his eyes as his phone vibrated. There were mountains all around him. He was about to reach Shimla in less than an hour. His roommate was calling. He picked up.

'Hey Ashu, where are you?' the roommate asked.

'I'm on the way to Shimla,' Ashu replied.

'What're you doing there? I was waiting for you yesterday.'

'I went to meet Anshu, but I didn't get the chance to see her. I've come here to find the only thing that is left between us.' With that, Ashu disconnected and switched the phone off. He again closed his eyes.

It was 7 am in the morning.

A few days ago (Anshu)

She opened her eyes at 7 am. It seemed she had not slept the entire night. She took her phone, thought for some time, and then dialed a number. She became sad again and shook her head.

She left the room without making any noise. She did not take anything; phone, wallet, nothing. She came out of the hotel and started walking. She walked for almost forty-five minutes. It seemed she was going to a specific place. She stopped when she got there. It was almost 8 am.

She stopped at a cliff of one of the mountain and looked straight anxiously, curiously. But her eyes were still, motionless. She closed her eyes

Present Day (with Ashu)

He opened his eyes. He got out of the taxi at 8 am. He gave all the money he had to the driver. He looked ahead.

It was the same place Anshu had come to a few days ago, almost at the same time

He stopped at a cliff of one of the mountains and looked straight anxiously, curiously. But his eyes were still, motionless. He closed his eyes

A few days ago (Anshu)

She was standing at the edge of the cliff. Her eyes were closed. She sniffed and said the last words of her life, probably to God:

'I tried to overcome but I couldn't. I tried to eject him from my life but could not find him as he is attached to my soul. Now my body can't take this pain anymore and I have to split my soul from my body. I know I'm doing wrong to all those who love me and care for me but I am not able to control my feelings. I hope you can understand me. I have only one request. In my next birth, don't give me the sort of heart that you've given me this time. Please give everyone the sort of heart that you've given to people like Ashu so that they don't get hurt. Because it hurts when someone plays with it. I know I'm committing a sin that is not defendable in your court, but if possible, forgive me. I know I'm being selfish now by going away from all pain and relations.'

Tears were pouring out of her closed eyes and her entire face was covered with them. She opened eyes, but could not because of the tears.

She wiped her eyes. Took a deep breath. Reached at the edge of the cliff. Raised both of her arms as if she was inviting someone to take her.

She did not fear death because all the pain and grief that Ashu had given her were about to end.

She closed her beautiful wet eyes and took a step forward and...

A sound disturbed the surroundings when her body touched the stones of mountains

Present Day (with Ashu)

He was breathing very fast and looking here and there curiously, anxious and bewildered. It was early morning and so the tweets of the sparrows were laced with the sound of traffic. He could not see really. But he knew what had happened here some days ago.

Manya had told him everything last night. Her Mom had been admitted in the hospital. She'd had a severe cardiac attack because of Anshu's demise. She couldn't be blamed. Which mother could see the damaged body of her sweet and lovely daughter? The doctors had kept her on ventilators as her heart had stopped working. She had lost the will to live with the death of her sweet daughter.

Moreover, he remembered the day when he had come here with Tanya. A crowd had stopped their car then because the local police had blocked the road as someone had jumped off from one of the mountains. Tanya and he had decided to turn back after hearing this bit of bad news.

Anshu was the one who had committed suicide that day. He was so close to her, but fate had not allowed him to see her one last time.

Oh Anshu, I was so close to you when you left, but... He stopped and looked down. His eyes were getting red.

A young, smart, positive, and attractive boy was standing and looking like an old man with a bearded face, shabby clothes, and red eyes; depressed and frustrated..

He looked down and closed his eyes. Tears started to flow down from his eyes. He was feeling the same pain now that he had given to her.

He opened his arms and knelt down slowly. The soil was getting wet because of the tears coming out of his eyes. He was breathing fast. He took a handful of soil from that place where she'd kept her feet for the last time before leaving this world. He shook his head and looked up.

'Now I understand everything. She cut her arm because of me and in return I got a lot of wounds all over on my body. I made her family suffer and in return my family is suffering now. I betrayed her and in return I was betrayed by Tanya. I changed myself, I tried to be good, but it was too late. Now I understand that I am getting only those things which I gave her. Betrayal, wrongful allegations against me and an insult for my family......
Please God, I request you to give me the heart which you have given to people like Anshu next time and to never ever give anyone the heart and feelings that you have given to me.'

He stopped talking and started looking in front, flashes of the past started taking shape in front of his wet eyes.

A Rainy day... Seeing Anshu for the first time... a beautiful girl... Proposing to her... kissing her... walking with her in the night...And then he stopped thinking... He was seeing just the good times... He saw her calling him after their breakup, calls which he had never picked up because was busy with Tanya... Her crying, crying a lot... In the end he saw her standing at the edge of the cliff ... She raised her arms and dived into the deep valley... Her beautiful body destroyed as it touched the stones... He mourned ...Mourned and mourned... very loudly... looking up... not caring if anybody was near... He mourned for her, his left hand was hitting his forehead and his head was bowed...

This was justified.

At the same place where she'd taken her last breath, almost at the same time…

He was mourning. Then he stood up.

He remembered what she'd told him once; 'It would be more romantic if you say anything filmy with tears and emotions in your eyes.'

Now he had in his eyes everything that she'd always wanted, but she was not there to see him.

Some lines from the Indian movie *Taj Mahal* came to his mind.

"Sabhii Ehal-E-duniyaa Ye Kahatii Hai Humse

Ki Aataa Nahin Koi Mulk-e-Adam Se

Aaj Zaraa Shaan-E-Wafaa Dekhe Zamanaa Tumko Aanaa Padegaa

Jo Vaadaa Kiya Woh Nibhana Padhega

Roke Zamaana Chaahe Roke Khudaee Tumko Aana Padhega"

("Everyone in this world challenges nobody comes after death,

However, you please come so that these practical people could see

The Pride and Joy of love, which you always carried for me

You have to keep the promise that you have made,

Even the world or Lord stops you, you have to come")

He came to the edge of the cliff, raised his arms as if he was inviting someone to him.

'I'm sorry Anshu… Please forgive me…'

And with that he threw himself into the deep valley.

Chapter 32

Ashu opened his eyes. He was in daze to see himself standing at the same place, though he dove few moments back.

An indication of radiant light drawn around the same place.

He touched his face. His clothes were looking new, white colored. Of a sudden, he turned back to find three people coming in his direction. That stirred fear in him. They crossed him. They were looking down into the valley and talking to each other, frightened. He was unable to hear them. There was complete silence around him, though they were verbalizing. He neared the edge of the cliff, shocked to see his bloodstained body lying on the stones below. He was stunned for a moment but then he smiled in disbelief.

He closed his eyes, breathed heavily. He nodded. A silence was spread everywhere.

He then witnessed himself standing at a contrived ambience where it seemed like as if the diffused light from the sky was spread.

He, in confusion, looked straight to find a wide, never-ending green steppe. After a thoughtful silence, he started walking, slowly, and surprisingly.

After walking for a distance, he began to see people, in white colored clothes, through the light.

No one was talking with anyone. Everyone was cloistered. Few were standing. Few were sitting. All were stolid. Everyone was in rumination. He stared quizzically.

As he moved a bit further, he felt a passage of electric current through the body as he found a half- perished flesh. His appalled eyes got a wide shape.

The flesh was lying at the corner. He looked up, closed his eyes, breathed heavily.

'Oh God! Where am I?' He drawled.

A known voice cut him.

'This is what you've chosen.'

He turned to his left, impetuously. He saw Anshu, wearing a white dress. He once again went in shock to see Anshu standing with him. She was looking in front. Her silky hairs were dancing around her face, flying due to the wind.

Her appearance was abnormal, and her expressions were dead stolid. Ashu was looking at her without blinking astonishingly. She glanced at him without turning her face. Seeing her his eyes filled with emotions.

Anshu asked: 'It's not good to be here.'

'I...I...This place...'

'This place,' Anshu took a little pause, 'move.'

She asked him to follow. He did the same. Strange faces were around them. A young guy was sitting, clasping his head. Seeing him, Ashu stuck in affright.

'These...This place...' He couldn't complete.

'This locus is fixed where the life ends. Just before the after-life journey begins.' She stopped walking, turned to him so did he. She gazed around. Her eyes were not even blinking. 'This place has administered an anesthetic drug to the veins of stranded ones. It is insensitive to any radiation. It is,' She took a pause before she could go again, 'all we have a guilt.'

'A guilt?'

She blinked once and began to walk again. She was stolid but Ashu was anxiously following her.

She pointed her finger at a young guy, 'He died in misconception of a better life post demise and see where he landed. There is no life after life.'

She shook her head, then shifted to a half-perished flesh, which was shaking. Ashu began to stare it, in affright. He turned to Anshu quizzically, did not speak.

Anshu spoke, 'It's been long he's stuck here. He's started to canker by degrees now. He also had gaffe that life is an infliction, then he left.' she shook her head again, maintained a distance from Ashu. She continued stating, 'how peaceful this place is. See all around. Nothing is moving. All souls.'

'What are they doing here?' He asked.

She gave him a fixed look, 'Wait?'

'For what?'

'Waiting for the time when we are destined to die.'

Ashu went in deep thought, narrowed expression. He reacted as if something struck him, 'Hang on! But aren't they already,' Anshu shook her head to say NO. Her behavior was still preposterous. He went on eagerly, 'but…'

'Everything is written. Every path passes through us, but at the prefixed time. Before that time, neither we find that way, nor the terminus. Neither of us had time to die. But still we left. To keep off the pain and defeat. And see where we landed,' she expressed utter disgust. She continued, 'self -annihilation is that sin that takes us into a place that is probably even worse than the hell. Our souls are marooned on this unmoved place where time does not move. This peace is hideous.'

She paused herself, seemed nervous. Ashu was trying to fathom her dictum as she went on again, 'We were better in pain, which if we had tried, and had a little encouragement, then perhaps, we would have overcome them,' she gave him a serious look, 'you shouldn't have come here. It's curse to be part of this herd.'

'Herd?' he queried, 'but I can see few only.'

Anshu looked behind him. He followed her focus to see behind himself.

'Well, turn around.' She uttered.

Ashu turned, did not find Anshu. He looked back again. Suddenly he witnessed Anshu standing there alone. But very soon, the number of people behind her began to increase. As far as his sight reached, he could see dead people. Mostly young girls and boys.

He kept staring them with mouth agape. He once blinked his eyes. As he opened, he found nothing but a wide green never ending esplanade. He felt someone beside him. He turned impetuously to his right, noticed Anshu's back. She was walking away from him. She stopped when he called after her.

'I thought we'll go along.'

She thought for moment before she could turn, 'If she had not done with you what you did to me, would you still have come to me?'

He couldn't confront her fixed look, bowed. She kept staring him.

He had a heart to say, 'I'm Sorry.'

She gave a little smile of disbelief, 'You are neither worthy of companionship nor let-off.'

They both looked into each other's eyes. Ashu bowed. She walked out then.

Ashu kept staring her until she disappeared from his focus.

He thought: 'If we don't get apology after a try, then we should understand that the hit to the aggrieved was not worth forgiving. Getting an apology is not what we're entitled to.'

He nodded.

And at last, he turned to the other side. He walked to near a big stone fixed there. He sat on it. His expressions began to fade out. Soon his face became dead stolid.

'Self-annihilation is a sin; I went to be cognizant of this fact when I had done it. My soul needs liberation now but dilemma is, wait time is indefinite.'

His vison was fixed to focus in front.

'Now I think, I was better alive. But…It's too late… Extremely late!!!'

The life of Anshu and Ashu ended in a sad and disgusting manner. Sad because they died and disgusting because of the way they died. Both became victims of emotional persecution and as a result they reached their ends.

Emotional persecution is a curse that comes into our lives when we are emotionally or mentally down because of the actions of someone close to us in some way.

We may be emotionally persecuted either as payback for something we did in the past, as Ashu was by Tanya. Or for no reason, as Anshu was by Ashu.

Extinction is the one and only reality of life. And both Anshu and Ashu went for the same. However, the way they espoused was nauseated. At last, Ashu paid the price for his betrayal of Anshu.

However, Tanya was still free and flying with her love, Armaan. She was laughing without any fear in her eyes. She was not aware of one thing – that the universe is round, and we reap what we sow. Who knows? She might have to pay for her betrayal in the worst way one day.